I0681966

Where Doubt Remains

Doubt Series Book 2

Sharon Johnson

Wicked Words Publishing

Published by

Wicked Words Publishing

PO BOX 712

Hamlin, PA 18427

Author's Note

This work is part of a multi book serial that is not meant to be read as a stand-alone. Each book will include a new pairing, but they will all lead to the fulfilling of the prophecy. This series will be mainly an M/M universe, but will include episodes that feature different pairings. Future episodes may include M/M, M/F, M/M/M, M/M/F, F/F. I promise you by the end every question will be answered and every bridge will be crossed, but it may not lead you to where you were expecting.

DEDICATION

To my loving and devoted husband and our amazing children - without your constant support I would have never completed this journey. You have inspired me to reach for my dreams by reminding me that the only failure in life is not trying. For all my friends and family who have not only supported my dreams but held me up during a trying year.

Hence the saying: If you know the enemy and you know yourself, your victory will not stand in doubt; if you know Heaven and you know Earth, you may make your victory complete.

Sun Tzu

Contents

Prologue

January 10, 2016

"My contact in the Council informed me that your identity has been revealed and that Nickolas was killed by that abomination. It might be time for you to pull out and let them catch that monster that helped you. Maybe that will allow you a chance to get out of the country."

Sara grits her teeth, struggling to keep her temper in check as she responds to the older hunter. She'd wanted the fucking shifters dead even before they'd murdered Nick, and now she has yet another reason to kill every single one of them.

"No. This is my mission. We all knew the chances when we started this, Nick included. I have plans for my pet, but he is a bit unpredictable. Now that we know for sure that Sean is the key and those freaks he is carrying are those of the prophecy, it's of greater importance that we don't fail," Sara responds.

So much has been sacrificed to keep this from happening, but the treachery of others has constantly gotten in the way. Shifters might have managed to trick most hunters into thinking they wanted to coexist peacefully, but she knows they are just biding their time before they turn on the humans.

"We also need to deal with those on the Hunter Council who have gone against the code and sided with the shifters. They've issued a kill on sight order on you and that shifter, so we can only trust those who have remained loyal," the older hunter warns.

Sara almost snorts. She hadn't expected anything else from that spineless conference of old men. They had shown their lack of character when they had refused to move against a witch working magic that endangered the public. Even after the sacrifices her mother had made to protect the witch's innocent human victims, the Council had done nothing to honor her death.

"I already have a plan in place to strike at those who have put their greed above the code. I have found that many of the Council members have business and personal relationships with the shifters. Once we expose their treachery, I am sure we will get more hunters on our side. They'll see that the planet belongs to humans--not these animals."

The older hunter laughs before sobering. "Your mother and grandparents would be so proud of the hunter you have become."

"Does Sean know about his mother's death?" Sara asks.

"No. It doesn't seem like anyone has pieced that part of the puzzle together yet." The older hunter chuckles.

"Good. So we still have an element of surprise. If we can get to his parents, we might have leverage to pull them both off of pride lands. If not, we go after the children. One way or another, we will get our revenge and save the human race at the same time."

"Happy hunting, Sara, and good luck," says the older hunter, his voice seeming to be an odd mixture of both proud and fond.

"Thank you. Good luck and happy hunting to you," she says, smiling as he ends the call. She looks out of her window at the New York City skyline, knowing it is almost time to leave the city behind and head home. Her wounds were mostly healed, and she would soon be ready to hunt her prey. They now knew who she was, but they had no idea the level of destruction she was about to bring.

Losing Nick had taken her by surprise, but they had all known what was at stake. All of them are willing to risk it all, and she will make sure he didn't die in vain.

There is one more move she needs to make before declaring war on those animals. Grabbing a throwaway phone, Sara prepares to set loose her number one distraction.

"Wow, I was starting to think I'd never hear from you again."

Smiling into her glass of wine, Sara puts on her friendliest voice. "Well hello to you too, Hugh."

Chapter 1

Sean ~ December 17, Thursday, Approx. 6 p.m.

Mother. Mother… MOTHER!

Sean struggles to open his eyes through the mind-numbing pain rolling over his body. In the distance he can hear someone calling to him. He doesn't recognize the voices, but something inside him urges him to go towards those sounds.

Sean almost wants to stay here, where he's safe from the pain and the woman who had once claimed to love him. Sara had savagely tried to cut his cubs from his abdomen… his cubs. Sean's mind clears slightly when he thinks of them, allowing him to feel that hands have returned to his belly.

Panic flares brightly as he tries to call to his cubs and will his body into action. He has to get away. He has to save his babies! Sean tries and tries to pull up his magic, but it won't come, his body is too hurt to fight back. For a brief moment his mind drifts to DeMatteo and what losing them would do to his mate.

Another wave of agony crashes over him when someone moves his body. It feels like he is being crushed by some kind of invisible force. He hears voices calling his name, telling him he needs to shift, and instantly he knows it must be his pride.

In his mind Sean screams in pain, because every jostle makes him feel like he's being ripped in two. His legs must be seriously wounded, because he can feel what must be DeMatteo licking frantically over the area. Sean tries again to call for his lioness, and his cubs, but she is missing, and they seem to be drifting further away.

Sean has never been a man of prayer, but right now he is calling on every deity he has ever heard of. Sean knows that he is dying, both him and the cubs are going to die unless he can find a way to use his magic to save them. Sean begins to pray the way Tien had taught him, hoping he has enough left to connect to his lioness spirit.

Timothy ~ December 17, Thursday

"Sean, can you hear me? Sean, you are really hurt. I need you to try to shift," Timothy coaxes as he tries to get around his Alpha. DeMatteo is prowling, growling, and not letting anyone get too close to the injured Alpha Mate.

"We need to move the Alpha Mate out before this whole place collapses in on us," Samantha advises.

Timothy races over to the pregnant Alpha Mate, ignoring the danger the upset Alpha poses. He knows DeMatteo's mate and cubs are becoming more unstable, and as he watches his brother pace, he asks, "Alpha can you shift back to human?"

DeMatteo shakes his massive head and chuffs angrily, and Timothy nods grimly as his brother confirms his suspicions. With DeMatteo trapped in his shift, Timothy will need to try to keep them both calm. He makes eye contact with Samantha, who nods her understanding and moves to stand in position on the other side of the Alpha Mate.

Timothy tries to call to the Alpha Mate through the pride bond as he checks over the massive amount of injuries inflicted on the Alpha Mate's body. Sean's body is littered with cuts and scrapes, but the large piece of wood protruding from his thigh is what has them all in a panic.

He doesn't dare do anything with it yet, but he carefully pulls out a smaller piece of wood that had been embedded in Sean's back. As soon as the obstruction is cleared, Samantha provides pressure to staunch the blood that erupts from the open wound. Timothy feels DeMatteo's agitation as he struggles to keep his lion under control.

"Okay, Samantha, keep pressure on the wound while we move him. Frank, you and John need to lift the Alpha Mate. Try to keep him level and lay him on the grass. We can't move him too far until we get his bleeding under control," Timothy orders.

He doesn't have time to worry about what might happen if his brother's control fails. He continues to talk to the Alpha Mate as they move him outside, his entire being focused on the Alpha Mate and the three tiny cubs he carries.

Being an Omega, Timothy is more connected to the emotional and physical well-being of the pride. He is programmed to care for his pride mates, and to aid in this, Timothy's bond with the pride is almost as strong as the

Alpha's. He can feel that the Alpha Mate and cubs are close to death, and the need to get him to shift is becoming more urgent.

If he cannot treat these injuries, it is likely that all four of them will be lost and with them they will lose their brother. Samantha no doubt senses the fragile balance, and her body is tense as they lift Sean off the ground.

Timothy can only hope that Sean can hear him. Their Alpha walks as close as he can to the group, but even in his lion form he seems to put his mate's needs before his instincts. Timothy can only pray that they don't lose another Alpha Pair tonight.

Sean ~ December 17, Thursday

Sean tries to hold on to that voice. He knows Timothy is telling him to shift, but he still can't feel his lioness. All he can feel is cold seeping into his bones. He can't move, he can't speak, he can't see anything beyond a dull light, but he can hear.

Mother… Mother… Mother!

The calls are growing more frantic as Sean searches blindly for the source. He can sense his body being moved, but he can't be bothered to resist. He needs to find those voices; he needs to save them.

He and DeMatteo have only just found each other. Sean had sworn to him that he would never be alone again and that they would be happy together. But now it seems as if life is going to deal the final blow by not only taking away his mate, but snuffing out the lives of their unborn cubs as well.

No, this is not happening. He is not going to lose his babies or his mate. Sean focuses on his magic, and he pours every bit of himself into the belief that he will survive. Slowly Sean can feel his lioness's presence, pacing just outside his reach, and he pushes harder. It feels like flames are burning through him as he drags his body towards his lioness.

Another wave of agony consumes him as something is ripped from his body, and it seems like an eternity before he is able to continue reaching for his lioness. The magic that Sara used on him seems to center around keeping him from his lioness, making the pain in his mind intensify every time he reaches for her.

When Sean finally sees where his lioness is, his fears are confirmed. Whatever magic that was used against him is centered completely on her. She is caged, trapped inside a cell and roaring in fury. Sean reaches towards the bars that surround her, but they glow and vibrate and seem to repel him away.

"God, please help me," Sean begs as he reaches for the bars again. He is going to die if he can't free her. He can hear the cubs' heartbeats as they begin to stutter, and his own heart beats with a painfully weak throb.

The familiar sound of DeMatteo's roar pushes him forward, and he grabs the bars and pulls. Searing pain rips through him from his shoulders to his fingertips, just before his lioness rushes out to answer her Alpha.

DeMatteo ~ December 17, Thursday

DeMatteo rushes forward as the beating of Sean's and the cubs' hearts begin to falter, his lion demanding that they save their mate and children. Both Timothy and Samantha jump back as their Alpha snarls and snaps at them.

Timothy looks over to his eldest sister nervously before speaking. "If Sean is unable to shift, there is little we can do to save him or the cubs. The wood has completely severed the femoral artery, and its position holding back the blood flow is the only reason Sean has lived this long. If they remove the wood, Sean will bleed out in seconds. Only his lioness will be able to absorb the critical injuries Sean has received."

DeMatteo begins to lick his mate's wounds, pushing at their bond. All he can sense is his mate's pain and the cubs' rising panic. Other than pained whimpers and shallow breaths, Sean shows no signs of life. Even wounds on his body bleed only sluggishly. Real panic begins to crawl up his spine as Sean's breathing becomes more and more erratic and DeMatteo can feel their souls separating.

The other shifters begin to whimper in distress as the Alpha Mate's heart stutters dangerously. If Sean and the cubs are lost, DeMatteo knows he will join them or have to be put down in a mercy killing. In a desperate last bid, DeMatteo growls out his demand that his mate submits and answer his call, before driving his canines deep into his mate's shoulder.

DeMatteo has to pull away quickly as Sean's lioness rips her way through his mate's injured body and immediately lets out an earth-shattering roar. Sean's body convulses as bones break and muscles bulge, hair sprouting into wild and untamed fur as the predator takes shape. DeMatteo can hear the others gasp as they take in the sight of the true form of their Alpha Mate.

Once the transition is complete, the lioness lays on her side and pants. DeMatteo can't help but let out a whine as he moves closer to his injured mate. This is the first time they have met in this form, and DeMatteo knows he needs to proceed with caution. An injured lion can be dangerous to approach; an injured Alpha can be deadly.

The lioness's eyes assess him as he approaches, and DeMatteo starts chuffing out in distress at the warning growl he receives when he gets close. The growl cuts off at the sound as the lioness scents the air. DeMatteo's eyes flash Alpha red as he moves closer still, and he drops lower onto his belly, showing his mate that he isn't a threat.

Sean's eyes blaze Alpha Mate orange in response. He whines high and loud, signaling his need for his mate. He sprawls and exposes his injured side, where another large piece of wood is still dangerously lodged inside him. DeMatteo calls for Timothy through the pride bond as he tries to comfort his mate.

"Jesus Christ! Samantha, help me! There is another piece. The shift must have pushed it to the surface!" Timothy exclaims as he gets a good look at the large piece of wood protruding from what would be Sean's groin if he were still human.

Even with all the blood, it's hard to believe that they missed it. Something that looks like it had once been a part of the floorboards was now embedded in the Alpha Mate's belly. Although it is less than half the size of the one they had pulled from his leg, the placement makes it far more dangerous. DeMatteo understands that this is why his cubs were dying; their little bodies had been fighting non-stop to heal the damage this chunk of wood must have been doing inside Sean's abdomen.

"Okay, Sean, Alpha? This is going to hurt like a bitch. Please don't maul me," Timothy pleads nervously as he grips the wood and pulls.

Sean's lioness's screams reverberate throughout the pride lands, and DeMatteo can feel through the pride bond as Timothy pours out as much calming and healing pheromones as his body can produce. Still his lion whimpers and cries out with the Alpha Mate.

DeMatteo struggles not to gut his brother when he hears his mate's pained yowl. Instead he pushes closer to his mate, licking any part of the man he can reach. The yowl soon tapers off to pain-filled mewling as DeMatteo licks over the wound to encourage it to heal faster.

"Okay, his wounds look like they are closing, but he will heal faster in the Alpha's den. DeMatteo, we need to move the Alpha Mate back to the pride house. Do you think you can shift now?" Timothy asks.

DeMatteo can hear one of their pride members running towards the clearing, but with everyone on the lookout, she is stopped long before she can reach the Alpha Pair. DeMatteo is already back to human form by the time Samantha brings her forward.

"Alpha! There has been an attack at the pride house!" Cassandra pants.

"Samantha, you and Timothy protect the Alpha Mate in the safe rooms. Take four others with you. I will call out when it is safe to bring him to the pride house," DeMatteo growls out around his fangs.

He doesn't wait for them to respond before shifting back into his Alpha form and racing off to the pride house.

Sean ~ December 21, Monday, 2 p.m.

Sean slowly opens his eyes. Disorientated, it isn't until he tries to recognize where he is that he notices the change in his vision. Everything around him has taken on a strange orange hue, but his eyesight seems to have magnified tenfold.

"Hey. Welcome back, baby," DeMatteo whispers as he gently strokes Sean's fur.

Sean tries to respond but can only make a sound that seems to be a cross between a yowl and a rumble. That sound is what finally clues him in to the fact that he has fully shifted into his lioness. Samantha and Tien had told him how massive his lion was when he had shifted during his tattooing. Unfortunately, he had shifted back to human before he woke up, so this is the first time he is getting to see his lioness. Looking down, he focuses on his paws - *holy shit he has paws* - as he extends one blade length claw after the other.

When he looks up again, he notices that his bulk easily takes up most of the huge bed. Feeling his cubs bright and content through their bond, Sean freezes instead of rolling onto his belly to savor the sensation of their purring and waves of affection.

Sean bends and twists to groom his belly, nearly doubling himself in half. They'd all made it through, and he feels incredibly grateful for surviving despite the odds stacked against them. They'd been drugged, kidnapped, and damn near shish kabobed, but somehow his tiny babies had saved them all.

Sean's body jolts when he runs his sandpapery tongue over one of his many nipples. They're sensitive enough as a human, and in this form, they're unbearably so. He makes a note to remember not to jostle those puppies too much in this form unless he wants a constant reminder.

The babies squirm and kick as he runs his tongue across his stomach, and he can see his skin stretch and move with the movement as he slicks his fur down. Once his fur is soaked, Sean notices the absence of his penis. Curiosity forces him to sniff lower, as he lifts his hind leg and moves his tail to get a better view.

Timothy had warned him that the animal spirit's gender is fluid, so they can manifest in any form. Sean is still shocked when he sees what he can only describe as his vagina, and he sniffs cautiously. He can only detect his own scent and the lingering odor of DeMatteo's seed there.

"Timothy would like to examine you and the cubs now that you are awake. Is that okay?" DeMatteo asks.

Sean's head snaps around quickly at the sound of his mate's amused voice. He has been so enraptured in his new body that he had forgotten that the other man was even in the room. For a moment, Sean wonders how his mate expects him to answer in this form, and then he remembers their bond.

He reaches through to his mate, flooding their bond with not only his approval but also all the love and happiness he feels. DeMatteo's smile is radiant as he returns the emotion through their bond. Sean isn't sure if it's because he's shifted or just because he missed it, but he is overwhelmed by the emotions flowing through him and the cubs as they kick out their enthusiastic reply.

Sean is surprised that he can hear Timothy approaching the den before his mate shows any sign of sensing his approach. Maybe being in this form has made his senses extra sensitive - *he would have to remember to ask about that later* – or maybe the Alpha is just distracted.

DeMatteo visibly flinches at the sound of the knock on the door, and Sean chuffs in laughter at his mate's obvious embarrassment as DeMatteo lets his brother into their den.

"Welcome back, Alpha Mate. I just want to draw some blood and do a quick checkup. We can do a more thorough exam once you're able to shift back. I know you are probably wondering, but you will be unable to return to human until your lioness is able to heal completely. You had some serious injuries, so it may take another day before you're healed enough," Timothy explains while drawing his blood.

Timothy continues to talk throughout his examination, and his scent and voice are so comforting that Sean can feel his lioness curling up in the back of his mind. Even the cubs seem to be at ease even with the Omega poking and prodding at him.

He doesn't realize he'd been lulled to sleep until he sees Timothy on the other side of the room talking to DeMatteo.

"I want to get him set up with an ultrasound as soon as possible, but as far as I can tell, everything seems perfect. I'll have more confirmation after I run this blood sample, but I am sure both you and the Alpha Mate will feel better once you are able to see the cubs," Timothy explains as he walks to the door.

Sean wordlessly agrees. Even though he can feel them moving, he knows he'll feel better when he can see them with his own eyes. The door closes with a click, and suddenly they are alone. Sean wishes that he could hold his mate, but as he looks at his paws, he knows that too will have to wait.

Sean feels jumpy, his lioness pacing in his mind. As he sniffs his fur, Sean can still smell the lingering scent of others and begins to groom himself again. It doesn't take long for him to return to cleaning his vagina, and Lord, he will never feel right saying that!

DeMatteo's laugh grabs his attention again.

"I'm guessing you would like to see yourself?" he asks. Caught sniffing and licking his own special super freaky Alpha Mate junk, Sean can feel his mate's continued amusement at his embarrassment through their bond.

Sean's ears flick with interest at the prospect of getting to see himself. DeMatteo chuckles as he climbs off the floor. After a detour to the closet to grab the full length mirror, he heads towards the light switch.

"There, that's what you and your lioness look like."

Sean twists his head as he tries to get a better look at his new form, but he is so large that the mirror can only offer him snippets of his body. If he could only forget the part about having a vagina, his lioness form would seem male in appearance. His mane isn't as large as DeMatteo's, but the lighter colored fur still clearly belongs on an Alpha male.

He knows he will need to grill Timothy on the ins and outs of his strange new body, but for now, Sean focuses on looking at his fur. It had felt wiry under his tongue, but his reflection looks smooth and flawless. Sitting up on his haunches, Sean can see his baby belly as it pokes out as a constant reminder of his amazing new life.

Sean lets out what he figures is his equivalent to a purr as DeMatteo scratches behind his ear. He could get used to this. The cubs kick out their agreement as he lies on his side to give his mate better access. Sean's eyes flash a vibrant shade of orange when DeMatteo begins to stroke his flank.

Exhaustion keeps pulling at Sean, the rhythmic stroking of DeMatteo's fingers seem to be connected to the part of his brain that is all lioness. He stretches his legs, careful of his new dangerous claws, and settles. He allows sleep to claim him once again as he and the babies continue to heal.

Chapter 2

DeMatteo ~ December 21, Monday, 6 p.m.

DeMatteo watches as Sean fades. Even though part of him wants to keep him awake and alert, the rational part knows that Sean will need at least a few more hours of sleep for his lioness to recuperate from the massive amount of blood loss.

The last few days have been exhausting. After finding out Hugh had attacked his little sister, DeMatteo had ordered around the clock patrols of all the pride lands. The entire pride had been stunned speechless when they viewed the tape of Nick's death. It was hard to believe that two people who had been considered family were responsible for the attacks.

When they returned to the shack, the Alpha Apex enforcers had been able to locate a few fragmented fingerprints, forcing DeMatteo to wait to get confirmation of the scent he had noticed all over and around Sean. If the results hadn't been so devastating, DeMatteo would have laughed at the suggestion that two humans and one crazy shifter could have caused so much damage.

But the fruit of their labor lies curled up asleep beside him. Sean's kidnapping and horrendous injuries are all the proof DeMatteo needs to keep him from ever dismissing a threat again. His own sense of superiority, as a shifter and an Alpha, had blinded him so completely that he hadn't seen the threat until it was almost too late. Because of his failure Sean and his cubs had almost paid the ultimate price.

He can't escape fault in this. How had Nick managed to get ahold of poison like that? Whoever had given it to him was powerful in magic enough to weave a spell that not only cut Sean off from the pride, but also bound his own magic and lioness as well. His Uncle is leading an investigation to find and prosecute everyone involved, but that does little to ease his mind at this moment.

These thoughts have been plaguing DeMatteo relentlessly, but he pushes them down as he takes in his mate's scent. The sound of four steady heartbeats calms his mind as DeMatteo slides closer to his mate. With his lion content to have their mate so close and whole, he finally allows himself to sleep.

DeMatteo races toward where he can feel his cubs calling to him, heading into the property his mate just inherited. DeMatteo lets out a roar signaling the others when he feels the familiar tingle of Sean's magic reverberating through the trees.

As he bursts through to a clearing, the sound of a vehicle heading over the underbrush catches his attention. But before he can give chase, the sickening sweet smell of his mate's blood floods his senses and sends him barreling towards its source.

DeMatteo can distantly hear the calls of his pride as they struggle to keep up with his relentless pace, but even they are drowned out by four familiar heartbeats coming from the barely standing shack.

Pushing on, DeMatteo leaps through what is left of the windows to get to his mate and cubs, unconcerned with any danger that may be waiting on the other side. The sight that greets him makes his heart lurch, forcing a pain-filled call to his pride from him.

Whoever caused the carnage is long gone, and there isn't time to hunt them down. All he can think about is getting his mate out of this building before everything else around them collapses.

"DeMatteo..."

His ears flick forward as he hears his mate calling to him, but he sounds so faint, as if he is using the last of his reserves. DeMatteo tries to shift back into his human form, but his lion is refusing to give up control, convinced that this is the only way to save their mate.

Even without his heightened senses, DeMatteo would know his mate is in serious trouble, and he grabs a piece of wood in his jaws.

"DeMatteo..." Again he hears his name sobbed, and it's hard for him to maintain control as the Alpha grows more desperate to reach their injured mate.

Part of what must have been a wall has collapsed in on him, and the scent of Sean's blood is thick. His body seems paralyzed by fear, and his mate and cubs are going to die if he can't save them. But he can't; he can't even seem to move.

Every passing second feels like an eternity as DeMatteo stands frozen, the heartbeats that have become the center of his life slowly becoming more distant. He wants to fight when hands grab at him and a distorted and faint voice calls urgently to him, but all he can do is watch as his mate lies in a pool of blood.

His body shakes as voices call his name over and over, and Sean's body seems to melt into the background as he is pulled back into consciousness.

"Wake up, DeMatteo!"

Hands shake him roughly, and the sound of his mate's human voice brings him back to reality with a start. DeMatteo knows his mate can hear the drumming beat of his heart racing. But he still tries to plaster on a smile, with the hopes of not upsetting his already fragile mate any more.

"I'm sorry, baby. Everything is okay. Just go back to sleep," DeMatteo apologizes as he runs his hands through Sean's hair.

These flashback nightmares have been making it impossible for him to get any quality sleep, and the fatigue must show clearly on his face because Sean studies him for less than a second before sitting up completely.

"Bullshit, DeMatteo! I thought you were going to shift right here in bed, and I can still feel your fear. That is not okay," Sean argues.

DeMatteo scrubs his hands through his hair again. He doesn't want to put any more stress on his mate, but he knows keeping secrets will only stress Sean more.

"Sorry, baby. It was just a nightmare," he admits gruffly.

It's not that his feelings embarrass him, but admitting to being so weak in front of his mate causes his stomach to clench. As the Alpha, it is his duty to protect the pride. They all trust DeMatteo to not only provide for them, but also to keep them safe. The fact that a human he had trusted and accepted had stolen his mate from him, on his own land, is proof of how weak and gullible he really is.

"Of me being missing?" Sean probes.

"Yes, but also of when we found you. Except in my dreams, I can't get to you. There is always something stopping me, and when I break free, you and the cubs are dead." DeMatteo pauses, not sure if he is ready to admit all of the things he fears.

DeMatteo knows that he is being selfish, but Sean is looking at him with so much love that he is not willing to risk seeing pity replace the look his mate blesses him with. It feels almost like he'll give the words life by speaking them and show his mate how unworthy of him and the pride DeMatteo really is.

The silence stretches on, long and uncomfortable with Sean just staring at him as if he is willing the man to speak. He is at a loss, his mind scrambling trying and failing to find the right words, any words. Any sounds he would have made die on his tongue as Sean climbs into his lap, seemingly unconcerned about DeMatteo taking his weight as he presses them together as tight as his swollen belly will allow.

Sean ~ December 22, 12:35 a.m.

"Hey," Sean hushes as he burrows deeper into his mate's embrace. "That didn't happen. You did find us. You found us, and you saved us. We aren't going anywhere."

Sean is not completely sure what is going on in DeMatteo's head, but the sadness leaking through their bond is enough to make him seek to comfort the Alpha. DeMatteo wraps his arms around Sean's waist. When he buries his face against his mate's neck, Sean tilts his head further, offering as much room as he needs.

"I know. I know you are safe and whole, but I think it might take a while before I'm able to let you out of my sight," DeMatteo confesses into his neck. Sean can only hope that the familiar scent of his mate and the cubs can help convince the Alpha that he has kept his pride safe.

"I am surprisingly okay with that." Sean sighs.

"You are?" DeMatteo breathes out, obviously relieved, ordinarily Sean would tease his mate about his clinginess if he wasn't just as desperate to reconnect.

"I am. I feel the same way; I just want to be as close to you as possible. There were times I wasn't sure I'd get to have this again."

"I will never fail you or the cubs again," DeMatteo vows, trailing kisses up Sean's neck.

The feel of the Alpha's lips on his neck has desire swirling low in his gut, the need to reconnect urging him to have his mate reestablish his claim. DeMatteo is still apologizing, pushing the words into his skin, and Sean is almost too distracted to understand what it is DeMatteo is confessing. Realization douses the flames, replaced with the need to comfort as his lust-fogged brain sorts out the words, and he pulls back to look at his mate.

"You've never failed us. We were attacked by people we never knew were a threat, but from now on we will protect each other," Sean insists, gently kissing DeMatteo's face.

It isn't hard to guess that DeMatteo is blaming himself entirely for what has happened, and that makes Sean angrier than he can explain. He knows that words will not be enough to erase the Alpha's fears. Instead, he works out a plan to show DeMatteo how much he loves him. Sean wants to show DeMatteo that he has never disappointed him, and he will continue to show him over and over, every day for the rest of their lives.

"I've missed you," Sean whispers into DeMatteo's ear, hoping to pour every ounce of emotion he feels into the words. His lioness rises back to the surface, demanding to claim and be claimed by their Alpha.

"I've missed you so fucking much, baby. You have no idea."

"Then show me," Sean challenges his Alpha, grinding his ass down onto DeMatteo's half-hard cock.

DeMatteo immediately stills beneath him, his hands tightening and relaxing rhythmically on Sean's waist. Sean can see the hesitation in his mate's eyes, and he wants none of that. Instead of asking again, he reaches down to palm his own erection, showing his mate he is more than interested.

Sean watches as DeMatteo takes a deep breath. He knows that his mate is battling to keep his lion at bay, wanting to protect Sean and the cubs. But after everything that has happened, Sean doesn't want careful or gentle. It's not what he needs. Every cell in his body is begging for the Alpha to mate him, mark him, and claim him as his own.

He can almost see the exact moment when DeMatteo understands what it is that he's asking for, and Sean can see his eyes flash brightly in response.

DeMatteo ~

DeMatteo takes a deep breath as he watches Sean stroke his cock, and he instantly knows he shouldn't have. The scent of arousal and his mate's slick is thick, going straight to his cock like a physical touch. He reaches out through their bond, trying to gauge his mate's condition, and he finds a fully healed lioness begging to be taken.

"Are you sure?" Feeling the waves of need pouring off the other man, he knows it's a perfunctory question, but DeMatteo feels the need to ask anyway.

"Please," Sean begs, and any reason DeMatteo could have had to deny him, evaporates with the dirty twist and grind of Sean's ass on his more than interested cock.

"Okay. Okay. Take it easy, baby," DeMatteo says as he grips his waist tight slowing Sean's movements, to bring their mouths together.

Even with his lion scratching at his brain, demanding they take their mate, DeMatteo is determined to take this slow. Too much has happened to have this just be a quick fuck, DeMatteo needs to make Sean feel all the things he can't find the words to express.

Sean hums against his lips, and DeMatteo takes that as his cue to deepen the kiss with quick swipes of his tongue. It's easy to fall into the steady drum of want he can feel building. For the first time in days, DeMatteo's lion ceases its relentless pacing in his mind, content to just sit here and taste their mate.

It doesn't take long for his mate to get impatient with DeMatteo's slow exploration of his mouth. Sean sucks on his mate's tongue hard and reaches down to stroke DeMatteo's dick. That plan is quickly derailed by the awkward belly hindering their movements. Sean's eyes flash brightly as he full out growls in frustration.

DeMatteo tries twisting his hips to maneuver around his mate's girth, unfortunately that results in Sean biting down hard on DeMatteo's lip in the process.

Hissing out in pain, DeMatteo pulls back and presses his hand over his cubs. "Why don't we just get on our sides? Don't want to hurt the cubs," DeMatteo suggests when Sean starts to roll his hips.

DeMatteo's cock brushes along his mate's hole, and he can feel his greedy little opening mouthing at the tip. DeMatteo quickly tries to help Sean roll to his side when he feels a fresh coating of slick pouring from Sean's hole, drenching DeMatteo's cock in his wetness.

"Fuck, okay. That might be easier," Sean agrees easily.

DeMatteo easily fits himself beside Sean, loving how this position allows him to place his hand on Sean's belly where he can feel children still growing, safe and protected. He reaches up to pinch a nipple when Sean starts rubbing his ass all over his cock, getting them both messy with slick.

"Please, DeMatteo. You won't hurt us. I need you," Sean pleads.

DeMatteo grips his cock hard at the base, swiping the tip around Sean's messy hole. Once he's gotten his lion back under control, DeMatteo begins to press in, using his free hand to pull Sean's leg up and out of the way. There is little resistance with Sean's natural secretions working both to ease the way and loosen the muscles.

Sean moans low in his throat as DeMatteo pushes in with one deep thrust. DeMatteo stills once he is balls deep, feeling the light flutter ripple through Sean's belly as the babies shift inside.

"Was that ..." DeMatteo begins.

"It's fine. They're fine, DeMatteo. Please, just don't stop," Sean interrupts, pushing his hips back and tightening around DeMatteo's cock for emphasis.

"Ahhh… Okay." DeMatteo moans, pulling back an inch before slowly rocking back inside.

The pace is slow and unhurried as DeMatteo runs his hand down Sean's side, mouthing on his neck, and making sure each thrust is deep and hard. He knows he's found his mark when Sean cusses and tightens around him, pulling his leg up higher. DeMatteo's lion growls as he picks up the pace, pulling out further only to slam back in.

"God, baby, so good. You're so fucking wet for it," DeMatteo moans around his fangs.

"Ugh… yes… Please, harder. I need you to make me come," Sean whimpers.

DeMatteo's claws slide out as he fucks harder into his mate, his lion climbing to the surface, eager to give their mate what he wants. A desperate whine escapes his throat as he spreads his mate wide, watching as his cock disappears over and over again. He can feel the tingle in the base of his cock as his knot begins to swell.

His lion is demanding that they reclaim their mate in the most basic way, and DeMatteo is helpless to stop it. He needs to reestablish his claim; he needs to ensure his mate knows that he will always protect him. DeMatteo's lion completely takes control, fucking up into their mate hard enough to shift him up the mattress. He would be worried, but Sean's frantic moans for more and harder, spur him on.

Sean ~

Sean slams one hand against the wall, bracing himself to keep from banging his head on the wall, as DeMatteo fucks him deep, he is sure he'll be feeling this mating for a week. He can feel his orgasm growing, and with his lioness mewling in his mind, he takes the hand that was bracing against the mattress and reaches down to stroke his neglected cock. Sean knows he is screaming, but there is no way to bite off the sound as DeMatteo slams into him, abusing his prostate.

DeMatteo's growls and the prick of claws breaking the skin tell Sean that DeMatteo's lion is the one mating him now. This thought has the lioness eager to submit, wanting to be claimed, marked, and bred by their Alpha. Acting purely on instinct, Sean tilts his head, exposing his throat with a moan.

"Please," Sean manages between clenched teeth. DeMatteo is pulling out until only the tip remains before slamming back in bone-rattling hard. Sean knows it's his lioness that is allowing him to take such a brutal breeding.

DeMatteo doesn't hesitate, biting hard and deep over the original mark restating his claim. Sean screams as he climaxes; caught between DeMatteo's cock and the bite, his orgasm hits him out of nowhere. His body clenches helplessly as DeMatteo's hips start slamming into him in a frantic pace.

He is so far gone that he doesn't recognize the stretching until DeMatteo is whining on every withdrawal. Sean clenches again, DeMatteo growls and slams in, and that's when Sean feels the tug against his rim as DeMatteo pulls back. Sean moans out desperately, just as eager to be knotted again. Needing his mate to knot, Sean urgently grinds back on that intrusion, making a point of clenching tight every time DeMatteo shoves his way back inside.

Without warning, DeMatteo pushes in hard and stills, his teeth still clamped tightly around the corded muscle in Sean's shoulder. Sean whimpers as the swelling rapidly increases almost to the point of pain, until the barbs located on the end of DeMatteo's dick shoot out and latch onto his prostate.

Sean shudders as waves of ecstasy roll through him, and he whimpers when his cock, which had deflated some with his orgasm, twitches back to life. It's too soon and there is no way he can come again, too bad his dick didn't get that memo. Pain overshadows the pleasure as his balls tighten again, wringing out another orgasm that's practically dry as DeMatteo starts grinding his cock in deeper.

DeMatteo ~

DeMatteo gently extracts his teeth from where they are still deeply embedded in his mate's delicate flesh, relishing at the taste as he licks at the blood that is slowly trailing down Sean's neck. He is close, so close, and he can't stop the words from spilling out of his mouth. His lion is chanting a chorus of *breedfuckmatemine* in his mind, and DeMatteo can do nothing but agree.

"My mate, mine. Gonna fill you up. Everyone is going to smell my cum leaking out of you," DeMatteo growls mindlessly.

His knot is still swelling, and when the barbs twitch, Sean bucks against him. That's it, he is done. He pulls Sean even closer, forcing him to be still and take it as he pumps what feels like gallons of cum into his mate. If he wasn't already, Sean would surely be pregnant after this mating. Sean wiggles in his hold and DeMatteo growls, urging his mate to submit. Sean goes still in his arms before relaxing, and DeMatteo hums in satisfaction.

"I love you, DeMatteo," Sean whispers, his voice scratchy from screaming.

"I love you too," DeMatteo answers easily.

Even with everything else falling apart, he knows that much for sure. DeMatteo kisses the back of Sean's head while gently rubbing his belly where their cubs are now kicking actively and sending waves of affection and happiness through their bond. The moment stretches on as they bask in the afterglow and the joy of just being together.

"Do you think they can feel us fucking?" Sean asks sleepily.

It takes a few seconds for DeMatteo's brain to try to begin to piece together his mate's question. Opening the pride bond, he tries to make out who his mate might have thought had been listening in. The pride bonds are stable; DeMatteo can feel each pride mate as they roam around, but no one seems to be reaching out to them.

"What? Who?" DeMatteo asks.

"The cubs. Do you think they can feel what we are up to? Cause right now they feel pretty excited."

DeMatteo shudders as his mind is flooded with that unsettling scenario. "Jesus fuck, Sean! Why the hell would you say that? I... I've never even thought about it. And I could have gone the rest of my life without that thought in my head."

"I'm just saying it looks like our cubs are going to love sex just as much as their dad!" Sean jokes.

"Sometimes you truly worry me," DeMatteo deadpans, hugging his mate briefly to take the sting out of the words. Sean just laughs, and DeMatteo is in awe of how much he loves the sound.

"Yeah, you love me," Sean retorts, pushing back further into his embrace.

"Yeah, I do," DeMatteo admits easily, readjusting his arm to serve as Sean's pillow.

"Mmm… Love you too," Sean murmurs sleepily as he wiggles further into DeMatteo's arms. Every movement tugs on his knot, causing DeMatteo's cock to spurt more cum into his mate.

DeMatteo closes his eyes and just enjoys the feeling of his mate pressed in tight. A sense of contentment and love floods through their bond from both his mate and the cubs. It will be hours before his knot shrinks enough for them to separate, but after almost losing their family,

DeMatteo doesn't feel the least bit guilty in indulging his lion's need for closeness.

Once he is sure Sean won't wake, DeMatteo grabs his phone to call his pride. Not only does he need to let the pride know that the Alpha Mate is well, but he also wants to send out a hunting party. The desire to provide for his mate and cubs is strong, but the need to stay close and keep them safe is stronger.

"Timothy, Sean has shifted back to human form."

"Excellent. Will I be able to come examine him now?" Timothy asks brightly, obviously still awake.

"No. He is still sleeping. Can we just come down to your office in the morning?" DeMatteo suggests, watching his fingers as they absently trace over his mate's delicate flesh.

"Of course. Come to my office first thing," Timothy concedes easily. After ending the call, DeMatteo quickly calls Samantha. It takes minutes to set up an elk hunting party. Once he is confident that his pride is secure, DeMatteo allows himself to drift with the scent of mate, cubs, and claim easing his lion into sleep.

Sean ~ December 22, 6:20 a.m.

His eyes open before sunrise. An orange glow spills through the blinds, and it feels like he's barely slept; a quick glance at the clock confirms his suspicion. Sean barely makes it to the toilet before violently emptying his stomach. His nostrils burn as he wipes his mouth, standing on shaky legs he gargles and is just about to brush his teeth when DeMatteo stumbles into the bathroom.

"Sean? You okay?"

"Besides puking my brains out for the last five minutes I'm just dandy," Sean jokes.

Sean looks up at DeMatteo in the mirror. His mate's hair is disheveled, but he is still easily the most beautiful man Sean has ever seen. It really is unfair that the man gets to wake up looking like a model when he is forced to watch as his once flat stomach rounds out to comedic proportions. For some reason, Sean is suddenly angry and depressed, and he frowns at the mirror as every doubt and worry in his head seems to be magnified.

"Are you sure you're alright?" DeMatteo looks so genuinely concerned that any annoyance is quickly squashed.

"I'm f…" Sean starts, turning to face his mate, but he has to stop mid-sentence before emptying what's left in his stomach all over DeMatteo's chest and legs.

"Jesus..." DeMatteo exclaims before he steadies Sean and helps him to the toilet as his mate continues to dry heave.

"Oh my god. What the hell is going on?" Sean asks as he retakes his position wrapped around the porcelain god.

"Morning sickness?" DeMatteo states, although it comes out more like a question.

His mouth fills with water as his stomach tightens again, leaving him gagging and bringing up nothing. Sweat forms on his forehead as he heaves over and over again. DeMatteo rubbing his back eases some of the pain, but if this is morning sickness, Sean is sure this will be their only litter.

"If it's going to be this way every morning, I might not be responsible for my actions against you," Sean warns honestly, knowing that DeMatteo can hear how true that statement is.

"I'm going to call Timothy and see if there's anything that can help. Can you sit here by yourself?" DeMatteo replies, handing Sean a wet cloth.

"Of course I can. It's not like I've suddenly become an invalid!" Sean answers, wiping angrily at his face. He knows he shouldn't have yelled at DeMatteo, but right now he just can't deal with the man's hovering.

He is trapped there, the threat of vomiting still fresh as DeMatteo silently cleans himself and the bathroom. The triplets start moving frantically and Sean nearly doubles over at the sharp pains as one of them seems to stick an appendage into his ribcage.

Every time he so much as winces, DeMatteo's body stiffens, and he no doubt wants to rush over. But sensing Sean's anger through their bond, he walks back into the bedroom instead. A few seconds later, Sean can hear him speaking quietly to who could only be Timothy.

"I'm sorry," Sean apologizes as soon as DeMatteo comes back.

"It's fine, baby. You're pregnant, and to be honest, I'm surprised that we made it this far without you being sick."

"That's it? This being pregnant thing might work for me if I just get free passes," Sean jokes. DeMatteo helps him up and immediately kisses him. He tries to pull back, knowing his mouth must taste like the inside of a garbage can, but DeMatteo just pulls him closer.

"We'll be fine. Get dressed. Timothy will be here in a minute." DeMatteo comforts him when he finally steps back, and Sean thanks every deity ever worshiped for allowing him to keep this new life he never knew he needed.

When Timothy arrives, he has little if anything to offer in a way to deal with the vomiting other than to say to stay hydrated and to keep eating. It takes all of Sean's willpower to keep from snapping out "thanks for nothing, Captain Obvious." The sentiment must have bled through anyway, since Timothy also explains that mood swings and crankiness might become a thing.

"Just try to get lots of rest. Also, it might help if you shift. Many shifter females spend a majority of their time as their lioness," Timothy offers as he makes his way out of the den.

"I need ALL the chocolate, stat. Oh, and some meat, rare, and maybe some tea," Sean demands as

DeMatteo helps him back to bed. Sean wants to scowl at his mate's look of amusement, but being wrapped in the blankets has him feeling drowsy.

After their mid-morning nap, DeMatteo practically carries Sean down to Timothy's office for his exam before skulking out of the room. Sean tries to calm his nerves as he sits on the examination table waiting for Timothy to do god knows what, but his mind was supplying him with a myriad of images that have him gripping the table to keep from flat out running.

Sean had asked DeMatteo to allow him to do this part of the exam alone. At first, his mate had been less than accepting, but it had only taken a few well-placed tears to have the Alpha agreeing to whatever he wanted.

Timothy had already requested Sean visit the clinic first thing after DeMatteo had called last night to say he had returned to human form. And after being called to their den, Timothy had decided that Sean needed a full examination. After what seems like an eternity sitting naked from the waist down on an uncomfortable table, Timothy walks into the room.

"So, Sean, how are you feeling?"

"Pretty okay, considering," Sean answers. Timothy just nods and writes on his pad.

"How have the cubs been moving?" he asks.

"A lot. They are really starting to get some power behind their punches," Sean complains, wincing as one of the babies decides to show off their newfound strength by kicking at his ribs painfully.

"Good. So I want to give you an internal ultrasound. Just to make sure everything is okay on the inside and we can get a look at those cubs."

"Internal ultrasound? How do you…" Sean's question is answered as Timothy pulls out a long wand that looks more like a medieval torture device than medical equipment. His heart rate speeds up as he watches the Omega spread a condom on the thing before coating it liberally with lube.

"Are you serious?" Sean gasps out, looking up at the Omega. If he thought being naked in front of the other man was embarrassing, Timothy has upped the ante tenfold by suggesting Sean let him shove a wand up his ass.

"Yes. This is the best way to check for damage to the passage. Now I'm going to need you to partially shift so I can insert the wand directly in the birth canal."

Sean tries to hide the flush he knows is climbing up his face as he realizes that the Omega needs to see his "vagina." Just the thought of anyone seeing his "vagina" is enough to make his head spin; call him old fashioned, but Sean really doesn't think that there will ever be a time when the fact he now has one will not freak him out.

"Don't worry, Sean," Timothy says as Sean lies back and opens his legs. After inserting the wand, Timothy starts to chat about ridiculous shifter lore.

"Do you mind if we don't chit chat while you have that thing inside me?" Sean grits out as Timothy shifts the wand, bumping against something inside him.

"Of course, Alpha Mate," Timothy agrees immediately, silently continuing the exam.

It isn't painful so much as uncomfortable as Timothy twists the probe inside him. Sean isn't sure exactly what he is supposed to be looking at, but the cubs seem to be wrapped around one another in what he can only describe as a puppy pile – cub pile - whatever. But Sean is disappointed that they are wrapped up so tight he will not get to see a clear image of the babies.

Timothy, however, seems to be hypnotized by what he sees on the video, only giving vague hems and haws before offering to print out the blurry images. Sean nearly falls off the table when Timothy says he can get redressed.

If he had thought his day of public humiliation was over, Timothy quickly disabuses him of that idea when he hands Sean a towel to mop away the lube and slick he can now feel sliding down his thighs. It isn't until he has the relative safety of clothes that Sean presses what has been spinning in his head since this morning.

"There is one thing that I noticed. I'm not sure if it's pregnancy-related or just stress because of what happened…" Sean begins, trailing off when he can't find a way to say how he's feeling without sounding like he is in need of a psychological exam.

"Well either way, why don't you just tell me? We'll decide how to go from there," Timothy eases, pulling off his gloves and sitting at his desk.

Sean stalls, taking more time than is necessary to button his shirt before blurting out, "I feel like an emotional trainwreck. Everything either pisses me off or makes me want to cry."

Timothy seems to consider his words carefully, watching Sean as he begins to pace in front of the office chairs.

"Well, that can be either or both. Pregnancy creates a lot of hormonal changes, and being a pregnant man introduces hormones your body has never had to deal with before. But I am certain that recent events have exacerbated their effects," he finally answers evenly.

"This morning I went from happy to depressed then to pissed off so fast, and I honestly can't even tell you what caused it," Sean admits, and just thinking about it now is making his eyes burn.

Ever since he channeled his best impression of Linda Blair, Sean has found that he just can't get a grip on his emotions. When he had found Sean sitting on the bed crying earlier, DeMatteo had dropped his fangs as he'd looked for the threat. Sean couldn't even explain that it was the fact that he'd already tried on at least three pair of his sweats before finding any that fit was what had reduced him to tears.

"That is all considered to be well in the normal range for a pregnancy. My advice is to do what your body tells you. Rest when you're tired and eat when you're hungry. Overexerting yourself can cause all your symptoms to get worse. And of course, come to me if you need anything, no matter how silly it might seem. You are not just the Alpha Mate; you are my favorite brother," Timothy jokes, throwing in a wink for good measure.

Sean squeezes his eyes tight and takes several deep breaths, blowing them out slowly rubbing his belly as he tries to ride out his latest emotional surge. Once he is sure he won't send the Omega into a caregiver meltdown, he slides into one of the chairs.

"Hmm... I'm not sure DeMatteo will be pleased to hear that." Sean chuckles.

"He'll get over it. You're carrying my nieces and nephews. That automatically makes you my favorite," Timothy jokes easily.

Sean smiles, feeling the easy acceptance and support the Omega gives. It does more to ease his nerves than anything else. Maybe he can learn to enjoy this new stage in his pregnancy with Timothy's help. He can feel his mate approaching long before he knocks on the door, and if he's being honest, Sean is surprised that he stayed away this long.

"Come in," Timothy answers and DeMatteo breezes in, immediately going to stand beside Sean. The babies react to the presence of their Alpha and promptly kick out their hellos.

"Everything looks great, Alpha. I am still unable to confirm their gender, but all three cubs are doing well," Timothy states, skipping the pleasantries in favor of telling the Alpha what he wants to know.

"That's fantastic!" DeMatteo exclaims in relief, bending over to drop a kiss on his mate's forehead.

By the time they are finished, DeMatteo and Sean both have their hands full of reading materials on everything from morning sickness to stretch marks. Timothy has also given them a new diet that includes a monstrous section on leafy green vegetables. Sean doesn't doubt that the entire pride will monitor his folic acid intake like it heralds the second coming.

Chapter 3

Richard Santiago ~ January 20, 2 p.m.

More than two weeks after Sean's kidnapping, the Alpha Apex finally arrives to deliver the news from the Council of Shifters. They haven't found Sara or Hugh, but they suspect that they hadn't fled far, leaving the Alpha Pair and pride exposed to the heightened risk of future attacks.

Not willing to leave anything to chance with Sean due in the next few months, DeMatteo wants to put the entire pride land on alert. They have already closed off most of the pride house for nesting, so the pride will provide house security twenty-four seven as well as patrolling the grounds.

"How are you two doing?" Richard asks.

"Good. Sean is still having nightmares, but we are working through it," DeMatteo answers uneasily. Richard doesn't miss the look that passes between DeMatteo and his mate, or the way Sean rolls his eyes at DeMatteo's glare.

It's obvious that they are speaking mentally, but when neither voice any other concerns, Richard decides to grill his nephew in private. There is no way the younger Alpha has survived all of this without some issues, but getting him to admit it might be a subject better left for another time.

"Good, that's very good to hear. Please let me know if there is anything we can do for you, Sean. Now if you're both up to handling Council business, in regards to the killing of Nick…"

"What? That was a clean kill. He was involved in the kidnapping of the Alpha Mate, a killing of a pride member, and the attempted murder of his own companion mate!" DeMatteo growls and the older Alpha has to suppress a growl of his own at his nephew's disrespect.

"Yes, and Carla ripped his throat out before anyone could question him. So we only have her word that he did these things," Richard challenges.

"What about the video of his confession? And Kim's statement, she was present during the event," Sean says calmly, but Richard can feel the anxiety pouring off the man in waves.

"Hearsay, and the video proves he knew something but not that he was actually involved. Anyone can argue that anything that Kim says is just the testimony of Carla's accomplice. You are both attorneys, so you know how this thing goes. And DeMatteo, you know that killing a human is something that is not taken lightly," Richard counters.

"Are you suggesting…" DeMatteo growls aggressively, obviously furious that his uncle could ever doubt his sister's word.

Richard raises his voice, cutting off DeMatteo's words before he can continue, "No. I'm not suggesting anything; I'm just stating why we had to investigate. The Council has discovered that Nick was a rogue hunter sent here on some sort of vigilante mission."

Unsurprisingly, his nephew's reaction to the news is explosive. Richard had debated not telling DeMatteo and Sean the full extent of the treachery they faced, but Tien had advised him that the real threat had yet to show itself. It's imperative that they have an idea of the forces they will soon be coming up against.

"Oh my god! You have got to be fucking kidding me. Nick was a hunter? So what you're telling me is he had been basically planning on killing my sister the entire time? How the hell did this get past the Council when he first attempted to join the pride?" DeMatteo seethes.

Sean immediately steps up beside his mate in an obvious attempt to try to calm the man, and Richard understands the implications of what he is telling the pair enough to give them a moment before he continues speaking.

"It seems as if his training had been done in secret. He was never ordained by the Hunter Council or recorded as a member of their order. This is in itself a violation of code, they are currently hunting down the man they believe to have trained him, but I am afraid that is only the beginning."

Richard waits until DeMatteo has visibly settled from Sean's presence before continuing, because he knows the bombshell he is about to share will send both men into a tailspin.

"The Council has it on good authority that Sean's ex-girlfriend, Sara Mitchel, is indeed a hunter."

Richard can sense the human's increasing panic before DeMatteo wraps his arms protectively around his mate, his hands resting on Sean's swollen belly trying to offer him comfort. It's good to see that they have already learned to seek each other out for strength.

"We now know that she is the person who helped Hugh escape by killing his guard. It is unknown at this time where they are hiding. The Council believes that Sean is at too great a risk. So they have issued a kill on sight order for both Sara and Hugh," Richard announces, even though he has his suspicions that someone close to the Council must have switched sides. It's the only thing that explains how those humans were able to infiltrate the pride.

DeMatteo's eyes, fangs, and claws shift as he growls low in his throat and Richard knows he won't allow anyone to get to his mate as long as there is air in his lungs. Sean's growl echoes his mate's as he clutches his belly tighter as if instinctively protecting their unborn cubs.

"We were able to learn why this hunter set her sights on you two, at least. The Mitchel family was one of the oldest and most respected hunter families. Their ancestors had been one of the humans that signed the original treaties."

Sean cuts in, "That does not explain why she went full bat shit crazy on us."

"No, it doesn't. But her paternal grandfather, grandmother, and aunt were three of the hunters who killed DeMatteo's parents. Her grandparents were caught and executed in accordance with the Shifter and Hunter Council orders, and her aunt died of injuries she received during the attack," Richard answers Sean, and he can see DeMatteo flinch at the reminder.

"That horrendous crime, and their unapproved use of poison, led to the entire family being excommunicated from the hunter community. It was her use of poison during Hugh's escape, and Sean's kidnapping, that helped us put it all together. Her father seems to have raised his daughter with the one goal of seeking revenge for his parents' deaths," Richard admits.

"So my ex is a crazy hunter that comes from the family that killed my mate's parents. This can't be a coincidence. She told me that she was sent to keep me from turning to magic. How would she know about my magic, and why did she care?" Sean demands, his voice raising until he's nearly screaming.

"It appears that her family had been deeply involved with shifter myths and prophecy, and had worked with your ancestors as well. As Tien had told you, many believe that your mating and upcoming birth will fulfill a prophecy of shifters 'rising up.' What that means exactly has been debated for decades," Richard explains, knowing it will lead to the reason he believes Sean is still alive.

Not surprisingly it is his nephew that asks the questions. "But why assume that it is our mating? You mean to tell me that we have a band of rogue hunters out to destroy not only my pride and me, but are also willing to kill my mate and unborn children to stop some prophecy from being fulfilled? I'm sorry, Uncle, but this is a little too crazy for words. How am I to protect my family from these psychopaths?" DeMatteo sneers, if any other shifter dared to speak to him with such disdain Richard wouldn't hesitate to put them on their ass.

It is all he can do to keep his lion from forcing the younger Alpha into submission, but if they are truly the destined Alpha Pair Sean would destroy him before he laid a finger on DeMatteo.

Richard reaches into his bag and produces the sacred text that had foretold of his nephew's life centuries before his birth. He had known that DeMatteo would fight against the notion that these events had been predestined to occur, so he brought the evidence that had been a closely guarded secret - even within the Council.

"It was foretold that an Alpha Guardian and Alpha Apex would rise from our families. Few know that the prophecy speaks of the joining of human and shifter into something new, a power we have never seen before. There are those, both human and shifter, who fear what that new thing may be. And like most things we fear, there are some that would rather destroy it before it ever happens."

"So what do we do now, Uncle?" DeMatteo asks.

"Now we prepare for the birth of your cubs and train. That is all we can do; be prepared for anything our enemies throw at us, and wait," Richard suggests.

"Wait? That is the best advice the mighty Alpha Apex can give me? Why did you even bother to show up with nothing of value to offer me?" the younger Alpha hisses out.

Richard waits impassively as DeMatteo paces and his nephew's features morph into that of his lion. Richard has not reached the position he holds by allowing Alphas to challenge his words or actions, but the fact that he can feel the true fear skating up and down his nephew's spine keeps his own lion from squashing the challenge.

"DeMatteo!" Sean interrupts, obviously trying to get DeMatteo's attention. Richard can feel the tension rising in the room, almost as if DeMatteo is itching to start a fight.

Richard is quick to interrupt Sean from confronting his mate; having the two at odds will do nothing to help their current situation. "No, Sean. Let your mate speak. He has obviously come up with a plan. Tell us, DeMatteo. Tell me and your mate what plan you've come up with to protect your litter?" Richard presses. While he loves his nephew dearly, his lion is not about to let a lower ranked Alpha cow him.

The situation is quickly swinging out of control as DeMatteo growls low in his throat at the challenge. Sean moves to stand beside DeMatteo, not being easily silenced. Richard can scent DeMatteo's emotion shift from fear to anger at his mate's perceived rejection.

"Alpha Richard, please forgive him. The last few months..." Sean begins but he is quickly silenced by the snarling DeMatteo.

Richard has no idea how this has turned into a dominance play, but he knows that his nephew needs to back down. Richard will never forgive himself if he is forced to attack the younger Alpha.

DeMatteo moves faster than even Richard could have anticipated, placing himself in front of his mate.

"Do. Not. Apologize. For. Me!" DeMatteo roars at his mate, growling out each word, his eyes flaring bright red as his claws slip out of his fingers.

Sean continues, clearly not realizing how dangerous this situation is becoming, as he seemingly aligns himself with another Alpha. Richard decides then that he needs to intervene before his nephew forces a fight. He eases back, putting more distance between the pair and himself while allowing his lion to rise to the surface.

"DeMatteo, please," Sean begs.

Richard decides to wait, watching as the human tries to talk some sense into DeMatteo before there is actual bloodshed.

"No! I am your only Alpha, and I don't need you to censor my words. You need to learn your place!" DeMatteo demands, grabbing his mate's arm and pulling him towards his body in a defensive maneuver.

Before Richard can move to show he meant no harm, Sean's lioness bursts through, the force of magic blasting through is enough to have Richard's lion bearing its throat.

"My place?" Sean asks dangerously as he pulls away from the shifter.

Richard never takes his eyes off the pair as DeMatteo deflates, immediately releasing the other man as if he was burnt.

"Sean..." DeMatteo pleads, but Sean cuts him off, seemingly uninterested in hearing whatever he was about to say.

"No, I am my own Alpha, and I am your mate," Sean growls, his claws and fangs slide into place. The room vibrates with magic as his eyes blaze in fury.

"Tell me, DeMatteo, who will follow the Alpha who doesn't realize that it is the loyalty of his pride that makes him strong? If you think for one second that you will command me, you have lost your damned mind."

Richard is stunned silent as Sean's eyes burn more red than orange as his lioness demonstrates her own incredible Alpha strength, intensified by a level of magic

Richard has never seen. He watches in utter amazement as Sean seems to vanish into thin air only to reappear on the other side of the room.

"Sean! Wait..." DeMatteo starts.

But before he can take a step, Sean vanishes again. DeMatteo starts to chase after his mate but Richard forcibly grabs his arm, allowing his claws to break the skin as they dig in.

"DeMatteo," Richard growls.

DeMatteo turns to face his face, growling low in his throat, with his fangs bared, as if he is ready to attack. Richard's own partially shifted face meets the other Alpha's, letting his bright red eyes bore into DeMatteo, as they demand DeMatteo's submission.

"Nephew, let him get his lioness under control. I understand your frustration but you have to trust me, your pride, and especially your mate; if you want a chance for any of us to survive what's ahead," Richard advises.

"Damn it, Richard! I'm sorry, and you know I mean no disrespect, but I cannot just sit in wait for some enemy to attack again. I almost lost Sean and the cubs because I didn't understand how dangerous Hugh was, and now you are telling me there are even bigger threats. I have to do something," DeMatteo huffs out.

Richard just stands his ground; he knows it is just a matter of time before DeMatteo sees reason. DeMatteo has to know he is right, but as an Alpha it's sometimes hard to back down. Richard understands that his nephew will not just sit back and wait for his mate to be attacked again, but running in halfcocked is the quickest way to get them all killed.

DeMatteo ~

"Yes, DeMatteo. You must keep your pride safe and protect your mate from these threats, but you must also keep him safe and happy in your marriage. We will all train and be on the lookout for any threats, but if you alienate and lose your mate in the process, what good will it be for you to remain alive?" Richard asks.

That answer is easy, DeMatteo doesn't want to live in a world that doesn't include his mate. Even if there was a way to survive breaking their bond, DeMatteo knows neither him nor his lion would want to. Sean and the cubs are his life. Scrubbing his face, DeMatteo knows what he has to do.

"How do I fix this?"

"That is the easy part. First, you will escort me to the door, and then you will find your mate and apologize for acting like an asshole," Richard jokes.

The honesty in that statement forces a laugh out of DeMatteo, his uncle has always been the type to go right to the jugular. So he is not even surprised when the older Alpha calls him out.

"Should I use those exact words?"

Richard taps his fingers to his bottom lip, pretending to think about the question before answering. "Yes, I believe that would be the most accurate description for what just happened. Then, you will explain all your fears and concerns and listen to his. And finally, you will come to an agreement on how to move forward."

Richard reaches over and pulls him into a hug, and DeMatteo lets himself absorb the comfort and affection his uncle is offering. With everything turning to shit around him, it is good to know that his family is here to support him.

"Thank you, Uncle. And I can't apologize enough for the disrespect I've shown both you and my mate," DeMatteo says into his shoulder.

Richard pulls away and looks at him, DeMatteo remembers all the times his uncle has been there for him. Not just after his parents' death, but his entire life. He knows Richard can scent his shame, and regret, for the things he's said. If anyone has ever proven themselves to be the kind of man DeMatteo hopes to become, it is this man right here.

"Don't apologize to me, Nephew, it is not needed. I have watched you grow from a cub and I know what your temper tantrums look like. But you might have some groveling to do before Sean forgives you."

"You think so?"

"Oh, DeMatteo, I know so. Tien has been bombarding me with her emotions, it seems as if your mate has contacted her for advice."

"Shit. Are you sure?" DeMatteo winces at the whine is his voice, but even his lion is cowering at the thought of a pissed off Alpha Mate.

"Oh yes. And trust me, I know my mate, you will be begging," Richard asserts laughing.

Sean ~

Sean hangs up the phone when he senses DeMatteo entering the house. At first he had been furious at his husband for treating him like some child to be commanded, but now he was just sad they had been reduced to this petty bickering. That was not the relationship they'd had before the kidnapping, and there is no way he will accept it now. Sean refused to let what happened dictate the rest of their lives.

After speaking with Tien, Sean was able to get control of his magic. He hadn't even known he could magically disappear and reappear until it had happened. He had just wanted to get away from DeMatteo before either of them said or did something they would regret. In a blink he had been at the door, and before he had figured out what happened, he had been in their den.

Sean turns and leans against the dresser when the door finally opens, but DeMatteo is moving towards him and speaking before Sean has a chance to figure out what he wants to say.

"Before you say anything, I just want to apologize. The way that I spoke was out of line. I was upset, but that is no excuse. I am sorry," DeMatteo explains, his voice cautious in a way Sean has never heard it.

"First, I want to say that yes, the way you behaved was wrong, but I forgive you. Second, I always want us to treat each other as equals. Third, and this one is very important, we need to be a team when it comes to making decisions for the pride, and our children. And finally, I want to apologize for losing control of my powers and storming off when I got upset. We have to be able to talk through our problems. So, I am sorry," Sean offers and it's true; he doesn't want them to just walk away when they disagree.

"You have nothing to apologize for," DeMatteo states immediately. "But I forgive you anyway," DeMatteo adds quickly.

Sean's lioness preens in the feeling of affection that DeMatteo floods through their bond. And he feels a wave of contentedness, knowing that their lives might not ever be perfect but that they would work through it together.

"So now we need to plan how to move forward and plan for the birth of our first litter," DeMatteo states as he pulls Sean's back against his chest, Sean's lioness calming as DeMatteo runs his hands over the swell of his swollen belly.

Sean feels all the fight drain out of him. His lioness knows that DeMatteo's instincts are being tested to the limits, and he doesn't want to let those bastards continue to taint what should be the happiest months of his life.

"Well, first we need to get through the next few months of my pregnancy. Even though it is amazing how little being pregnant has affected me. I mean, except for the weight gain and morning sickness, there really hasn't been anything major," Sean adds as he squirms to get comfortable.

DeMatteo chuckles at that, not daring to contradict his blatant lie, and Sean is reminded of why he is so in love with his mate. "Okay and I've been a… bit emotional," Sean concedes.

"A bit," DeMatteo agrees.

DeMatteo shuffles them around until he is sitting on the bed with Sean between his legs, and Sean relaxes further when DeMatteo's deep rumbling vibrates his back. DeMatteo starts to rub his shoulders, and Sean is surprised to feel how tight his muscles are when he presses in.

"You know you might have just cursed yourself, right?" DeMatteo asks after a few minutes of silence. Sean is so unprepared for the comment that it takes him a minute to remember what he had been saying.

"Yeah? Why's that?"

"Most shifters don't really feel the effects of pregnancy until the last month or two. It is nature's way of keeping the lioness safe in the wild. A sick female would be an easy target for other predators, not to mention she would slow the pride down."

"Well that is great. Now I have that to look forward to." Sean exhales. His body feels floaty and warm as DeMatteo continues to render him boneless.

Sean shifts his weight as the cubs press against his hips, and he is greeted with DeMatteo's hardened length being pressed firmly on his back. Sean's heart rate flutters as his cock twitches in interest. Since he had suffered during their fight, Sean decides it's only fair that he's treated to make-up sex.

Sean slowly presses his ass back further, making sure to shimmy enough that he massages DeMatteo's cock in the process. A slow smile stretches across his face when DeMatteo thrusts up against him in response.

DeMatteo ~

DeMatteo lays his hands on Sean's shoulders, staying motionless for a few minutes and relishing the feel of Sean sinking into his embrace. DeMatteo knows that he needs to work with his mate, but his lion wants to lock Sean in their den: keeping him safe.

DeMatteo starts back up with the massage when Sean begins to squirm. His cock is perking up with every shift of Sean's hips, but DeMatteo refuses to try to push for sex. He feels lucky that his mate is allowing this amount of contact so soon after their blow up.

Even though the fight was more his fault than anything, and even though he knows it's wrong, DeMatteo still feels possessive and protective of the man tucked up under him. He knows if Sean even suggests for one moment that he would allow it, DeMatteo would find them a den deep in the pride lands, and no one would catch a sight of them until well after the cubs were weaned.

DeMatteo winces as Sean shifts again. His cock is getting so hard it's almost painful, but a careful sniff of Sean's neck confirms that all his mate is feeling is contentment. Sean shifts again, and this time DeMatteo can't help but to hiss as his cock is wedged between his abs and Sean's back. He fights to not thrust up against him, until the scent of arousal curls in his nostrils.

This time when Sean pushes back, DeMatteo doesn't even attempt to hold back, shoving his hips up, desperate for friction. He slides his hands down Sean's arms, feeling the new sexual tension as it grows. Sean moans and wiggles, making it increasingly difficult for DeMatteo to take his time.

DeMatteo slides his hands across his mate's belly before reaching low to slide them up his sweatshirt. He is careful when sliding his thumbs over Sean's chest, knowing his nipples have been growing more sensitive lately. DeMatteo caresses his mate's protruding nipples through his shirt. The muscles that used to define his chest are now more rounded and full. Sean's head drops to his shoulder, and DeMatteo takes the opportunity to bite gently on his mating mark.

"Hey, let me see you," DeMatteo suggests as he pulls his hands free of the fabric. Sean twists his neck, as if searching, and DeMatteo is quick to provide. Sealing their lips together and thoroughly fucking his mouth. When they finally pull apart, Sean looks drugged, and DeMatteo is in awe of how beautiful his mate looks like this.

"Fuck, okay," Sean slurs, struggling to get back on his feet. DeMatteo is smart enough to realize that laughing now would be at his own peril, but the man is absolutely adorable. Not that Sean would appreciate that assessment.

"Here, baby, let me," DeMatteo purrs.

"Thank you." Sean lifts his arms obediently, and DeMatteo caresses each inch of skin he reveals as he pulls the soft material up and away from his body.

DeMatteo quickly pulls the sweatshirt over Sean's head, tossing it carelessly before dropping to his knees. He presses his ear to the growing swell where his children are growing safe, protected inside his mate's body. Their heartbeats are steady and strong, and one of his sons kicks out a greeting against his lips as he places a gentle kiss there.

"You are such a sap, 'Alpha,'" Sean teases as he looks down, but DeMatteo can feel the strum of happiness that he is projecting through their bond. Feeling playful, DeMatteo flashes his eyes at his mate and growls, grabbing his sweats and pulling them down roughly.

"Careful, mate," DeMatteo growls, letting his lion out to the surface as his claws lightly rake down Sean's thighs.

The results are immediate. Sean's scent of arousal spikes as a new scent of lubricant swells from his hole. DeMatteo's fangs drop as he tries to focus on pulling back in his claws, but his cock is pulsing, desperate to be inside.

"I don't think I'm gonna be able to take you gently," DeMatteo warns around a mouthful of fangs. His hands are groping, pulling Sean's cheeks apart, enjoying the eager, enticing way Sean is shoving his hard cock in his face and leaving smears of pre-come on his cheek.

"I don't need you to be gentle, Alpha. I need you to fuck me," Sean moans, his eyes bright orange: proof that his lioness is eager to claim and be reclaimed by her mate.

DeMatteo pulls his own shirt off as he stands. He doesn't need any more invitation; his mate needs, and he is eager to provide. DeMatteo all but rips off his pants, watching as Sean crawls into their bed, displaying his eager hole that is shiny and dripping with slick. He is not willing to take his eyes off Sean as his mate spreads his legs obscenely, and everything is discarded hastily.

"I want you to knot me," Sean begs breathlessly.

"Look at you, baby. You're so wet," DeMatteo comments absently as he climbs behind Sean.

"So embarrassing," Sean complains.

"You never have to be ashamed with me, love. You're perfect, made just for me. I could have never wished for a more perfect mate," DeMatteo praises. Sean's huff of laughter is muffled by his arm.

"Such a sap."

DeMatteo begins trailing his lips down Sean's spine, nipping lightly at each vertebra, wanting to worship every inch of skin he can reach. Sean moans and pushes back wantonly as DeMatteo massages his hips. He squeezes each cheek, watching in starved fascination as the pale skin blushes beautifully under his hands.

Pulling Sean's cheeks further apart, DeMatteo is drawn in by how his hole gapes slightly as more slick wells to the surface. Pushing slightly with his thumbs just to watch that hole open wider, DeMatteo sees he won't even need to prep him; Sean's body is eagerly opening for him.

"DeMatteo, please." Sean whimpers, pushing back wordlessly to ask DeMatteo to give them both what they need.

DeMatteo has no interest in denying his mate. Spreading him wide, DeMatteo eagerly laps at his hole. Sean pushes back against his mouth, moaning words that make no sense but still egg him on. Pointing his tongue, DeMatteo pushes in as far as he can reach, needing to get more of the sweet slick oozing around his tongue.

"Fuck, fuck, fuuuck!" Sean chants, trying to spread his legs.

DeMatteo takes that for the invitation that it is and lets his lion closer to the surface. His tongue shifts, longer, thicker, and rougher; Sean keens, bucking wildly and forcing him to grip harder until his claws break the skin.

DeMatteo growls deep in his chest as Sean fucks back against his tongue. The sounds coming from him are high and desperate and going straight to DeMatteo's dick. Forcing his claws back in, DeMatteo rubs his now blunt thumbs against his mate's rim. He presses in, stretching him so wide DeMatteo can see his pink walls, drenched in his own slick and spit.

"DeMatteo, fucking please!" Sean begs breathlessly, his own claws digging into the mattress and ripping the sheets as he writhes around.

The sight and smells combined with his mate's begging is what finally forces DeMatteo to pull back and push in abruptly, burying himself to his already swelling knot. Sean whimpers, his legs shaking from the hurried penetration, and that is enough to snap DeMatteo out of the mating haze.

"Shit. Sorry, baby," DeMatteo apologizes, running his hands along Sean's side and hoping to ease any discomfort.

"No, no, it's okay." Sean groans. His voice is strained and the burst of salt in the air signals to DeMatteo that his mate is crying.

"Damn it. The babies…" DeMatteo says as he eases back. Even his erection is beginning to sag with the thoughts of how he could have injured his mate and cubs. Sean clamping down on his dick suddenly was enough to make the Alpha wince.

"Don't pull out. I'm fine, the babies are fine. I liked it," Sean says seriously.

DeMatteo is hit with sensations as his mate pushes what he is feeling through their bond. It is intense, almost like being on a highly sexual feedback loop.

"Are you sure?" he asks again, unconvinced, and is rewarded by Sean shoving back on his cock hard and growling. DeMatteo can't help but to grind against his mate's ass in response to the aggressive move, his lion all but demanding that they satisfy their mate.

"I am not fragile; you're not going to break me." Not wanting to take any more chances, DeMatteo eases to his side, taking Sean with him. From there it's easy to reach around and give his cock a few tugs, Sean had lost some of his erection but DeMatteo is quickly getting him back to full hardness.

"Okay, baby. God, you are still so tight. It's like you're strangling my dick. Not sure how long I'm going to last." DeMatteo pants, giving a few long, deep strokes. Sean immediately starts moving with him. DeMatteo has to keep the pace slow or there is a real chance he'll pop his knot way too soon.

"I'm not going to last long, want to come on your knot," Sean gasps out. The feeling of DeMatteo's knot as it barely catches his rim is getting him there in record speed.

If DeMatteo wasn't equally as far gone, Sean would have been embarrassed to be so close to coming.

DeMatteo grinds in deep with even strokes, lighting up his prostate. Gripping the sheets, Sean pulls his leg up higher, needing to feel it as deep as possible. "Don't stop, I want you to fuck your cum into me."

DeMatteo's hand joins his, pushing his leg up that much higher, and slams in harder, grinding deeper as if he is trying to shove his balls in as well. "Jesus, you can't say shit like that." Sean can feel the knot swelling impossibly large, reducing DeMatteo to short grinding motions.

"Fuck, Sean. I'm gonna fucking knot you!" DeMatteo exclaims, pushing his dick in as far as it can possibly go before stilling. Sean can only whimper and moan as his balls draw up tight, the knot in his ass locking them in place.

Sean feels the second the barbs latch onto his prostate, and he is done; his body locks up tight as his orgasm is forced out of him. DeMatteo is growling, his claws pricking Sean's thighs before he strikes, driving his fangs deep.

Sean almost blacks out from the pleasure coursing through him as their bond flares brightly. He can feel it as DeMatteo releases what feels like endless streams of cum painting his insides. No doubt the bed would be drenched if DeMatteo's knot didn't have him plugged up tight.

After what seems like an eternity his body stops shaking, and Sean can focus on DeMatteo who is still making abortive thrusts, grinding and whispering the filthiest words into his flesh: a non-stop mantra of, "So good for me. Gonna fucking drench you in cum. Breed you so good, such a perfect little mate," as he rides out his orgasm.

The words soon taper off and are replaced with tiny kisses along his shoulder. "Hey. Welcome back, baby," Sean whispers when DeMatteo starts to gently rub on his belly, it has quickly become the Alpha's favorite way to relax.

"Hey," DeMatteo answers, blissed out.

Between the passionate love making and the tense night, Sean is not surprised that he can feel the Alpha's exhaustion seeping through their bond. Luckily the remote for the lights is right beside him, so Sean barely has to reach to get it.

DeMatteo's sleepy, "Love you, Sean," is the last thing Sean hears as he tucks in close to his Alpha and let's sleep pull him under.

Chapter 4

February 3, 7 a.m.

Sean takes back every time he has ever told a woman how beautiful she looks pregnant and every joke he's ever uttered about how much women complain. The last few weeks of this pregnancy have left him tired, bloated, and miserable.

After getting out of bed for what has to be the millionth time, Sean makes his way downstairs to find something to eat. Halfway down, his mind supplies him with a sudden craving for elk. Lately his need for meat, the bloodier the better, has been well past the point of alarming.

"Where the hell is the elk I put in here yesterday? I swear to god if someone ate my food, I will…" Sean complains to himself as he makes his way back to the staircase.

"DeMatteo!" Sean yells towards the stairs. There is no way he is attempting to heft his ass back up the stairs. Rubbing his back, he hears DeMatteo's heavy footfalls as he hurries down the hall.

Sean knows that his body is well on the mend since now he is hit with constant cravings. Timothy assured him that this was all perfectly okay, but it is starting to border on the line of obsessive. He can't even sleep through the night without sending DeMatteo out for supplies.

"Sean! Is everything okay?" DeMatteo asks, worry lining his adorable face as he searches Sean for anything that might explain why his mate is screaming for him. When he finds nothing, he just arches his eyebrow and waits. He has become accustomed to Sean's demanding nature.

"No, I want some elk. I know I left some in the refrigerator, but I can't find it." Sean whines as he walks back into the kitchen, the triplets resting heavily on his hips.

DeMatteo sighs, shaking his head, which only makes Sean unreasonably upset. "Elk? Babe, you sent me to get it for you last night, remember?" he asks, exasperated, and Sean suddenly has to blink back the burning in the back of his eyes.

"Can you get me some more?" Sean asks hopefully, blinking back the tears that are already threatening to escape.

Between his emotions and the food cravings, Sean has been an emotional, hungry mess, and everyone in the pride has been tiptoeing around the pride house trying to not endure the wrath of their Alpha for upsetting the Alpha Mate. It's no wonder why no one really ever talks about this part of pregnancy. If they did, the rise in shifter population might come to a screeching halt.

Between hot flashes, dizziness, swollen ankles, and mood swings, it's a wonder anyone ever did this more than once. And since DeMatteo was the one who managed to knock him up, something that shouldn't even been a thing, he can damn well give him whatever the hell he wants.

DeMatteo waves towards the fridge helplessly. "Babe, can I just make you some steaks? We have bacon, ham…" He tries offering in concession. Sean's face goes through a range of emotions before settling on wounded, and DeMatteo knows he's done for.

"Please… DeMatteo. I'll eat a little while you're gone, but the babies really want elk meat. It's one of the few things that doesn't give me horrible heartburn." It's a dirty ploy, but Sean makes sure to rub his belly and sound as needy as possible, knowing that the Alpha's need to provide will get him what he wants.

DeMatteo rolls his eyes and makes a big production of rubbing his hands across his face before relenting, just like Sean knew he would. "Okay. Fine, just make sure you eat something light at least." He is up and heading out the door before Sean can tell him to stop being such a drama queen; it's not like he is the one who is pregnant.

"Yes, dear. Have I told you lately what a wonderful Alpha you are?" Sean teases. Heading back to the fridge, Sean can feel DeMatteo's amusement as he shifts and heads out into the pride lands to catch Sean's breakfast.

Half of the ham is already demolished when Carla joins him in the kitchen. She eyes him carefully before reaching into the fridge grabbing the milk. "Good morning. Would you like something to drink?" she asks.

"Yes, thank you. You're not eating?" Sean replies, biting the meat directly off the bone.

It's likely he'll finish the entire thing so he has learned to skip false modesty and just eat to his heart's content. Carla continues to watch him, amusement mixed with disgust twisting her face as he adds strawberries to the mouthful of ham he's chewing. When she shakes her head at his questionable combination, Sean almost regrets coming out of the room around his judgmental in-laws as he finishes the plate.

"I would eat, but it seems my Alpha Mate has eaten my ham." Carla cackles, her smile taking any sting out of the words.

"Shit, I'm sorry, Carla." Sean knows his face is flaming in embarrassment, and he can already feel his eyes beginning to burn as tears well up in them.

It wouldn't have been so bad if this was the first time it happened, but just yesterday he had managed to snag Samantha's pasta and Mary's last piece of pie. He'd be lucky if he ever saw his feet again after this pregnancy.

"Hey, Sean, it's okay. I was just fucking with you," Carla soothes and Sean isn't sure if she scents his tears or can feel his impending breakdown, but knowing she knows has him sobbing uncontrollably.

Before he can wipe his nose, Sean is being gathered up in deceptively strong, small arms and rocked gently. He will deny it to his dying day, but Sean can feel his lioness purring in his head at his pride mate's caring.

"I'm fine," Sean tries, his laugh shaky in his own ears. Carla looks ready to object so he adds, "I'm telling you, pregnancy is not for the weak." This seems to calm his sister-in-law slightly, though she eyes him warily before releasing him and heading to the fridge.

"How about I make you something to wash down all that ham?" Carla asks, and Sean is eternally grateful that she is willing to pretend his meltdown never happened. The conversation is light and Sean settles in his seat as Carla grabs a slab of bacon from god knows where and proceeds to whip up some eggs.

Out of nowhere, Carla asks, "Have I ever told you about the time DeMatteo got so drunk he wound up waking up half the pride as he ran around roaring buck ass naked halfway through the pride lands?"

"No, but now I need all the details," Sean answers after almost choking on air.

DeMatteo ~

By the time he makes it to the porch, DeMatteo can hear Sean and Carla laughing in the kitchen. Under normal circumstances, the Alpha wouldn't hesitate to drag his kill into his mate, eager to prove his ability to provide for his cubs. But with his mate's explosive mood swings DeMatteo is hesitant to do anything that might cause a shift in his currently happy one.

So no one could really fault him for taking his time to cut the animal apart outside, it's not that he was hiding, more like avoiding.

"Hey, baby. Have a good hunt?" Sean asks.

DeMatteo eyes Sean warily when he comes back awhile later, dragging parts of the freshly killed elk into the kitchen. There is little doubt his mate had a minor breakdown while he had been gone. Their bond ensured that DeMatteo had felt every bit of Sean's mood swings.

"Yes, I got an elk. I just need a bit to finish dressing it, but I see you've already managed to find yourself some breakfast," DeMatteo answers carefully.

DeMatteo had almost abandoned the hunt completely when a burst of overwhelming sadness had flooded his mind. Now the bond is filled with happiness, the mood switching so quickly DeMatteo feels whiplash. He is almost tempted to ask what had happened, but the Alpha is smart enough to not bring it up when he sees them still laughing over their shared plate of eggs and bacon.

"Yes, and your sister has been kind enough to hang out with me and entertain me with some very interesting stories about your misadventures in streaking. Care to fill in the blanks?"

Hugh/Chris ~ February 3, 12 p.m.

Hugh arrives at the Ballard Locks waterway a little before noon. Sara has given him instructions to meet with someone named Chris; this human would have the items he needs to finish the packages. He had been careful to stay on the outskirts of the state, making sure no one from the pride would easily catch his scent.

His lion paces restlessly in his head as he watches the endless parade of tourists, all gathered around the docks. With little warning, his lion is alert, sensing danger. Hugh scans the crowd looking for anyone familiar, trying to be discreet as he scents the air.

His eyes flash and he almost drops his claws when a hand clamps on his shoulder. Spinning around, Hugh finds himself face to face with a human. Old age does nothing to hide the fact that this man is a threat. Refusing to back down, Hugh lets his fangs drop so only the man looking at him, with an air of disapproval, can see them.

"Hugh, I assume? This is hardly the place to let your temper get the better of you. I am Chris, by the way," the older man chides as he turns his back and begins to walk down the sidewalk.

Chris is an average-sized man who had been somehow able to sneak up on both Hugh and his lion. This human had somehow moved without making a sound, and instead of snatching back his hand at Hugh's thinly veiled threat, the human's grip tightens when he sees the glint of fang. Hugh's lion is confused and unsure of how to proceed. This human doesn't react like prey as he turns his back on the lion.

Without slowing or turning to make sure he is being followed, the older man calls out, "You'll need to follow me, young man, if you have any hopes of finishing your task on time."

He stands there for a moment, watching this human dismiss him without the faintest flutter of his heartbeat, before following him as they make their way back to the parking area. They end up in one of the buildings. It is abandoned, but this human somehow has the keys.

Hugh decides that not only would he need to be careful around this "Chris," the man is clearly dangerous, but the most frightening thing Hugh realizes as he watches the man start handling the packages, as if they weren't highly-charged explosives, is that this man is completely insane.

Chris ~

Chris knows the shifter is wary of him. It's obvious that this one is no hunter. His body language screams scared, nervous, weak, and prey. He is not worried about anyone interrupting them. This is one of the many buildings and safe houses he owns in the area.

Using one of his many businesses made it ridiculously easy to get the C4 and detonation cords needed to pull off the job, but Chris hadn't been sold on trusting some dumb animal to carry out this crucial step. Once both targets are hit, it will be more than enough to get the Council moving in. He just needs enough of a distraction so he can get into the archives and find that missing pack.

Chris smiles as he installs the detonator cord into the explosives. The shifter eyes him nervously. And to think many elders on the Human Council argue that these animals are the height of human evolution, which is a heresy made only more insulting by this cowardly lion.

He is man enough to admit that Sara's plan is perfect. Using this shifter will ensure that when they bring in the enforcers they will be led to the right path. It even stands to reason that the enforcers might call for the pride's extermination, effectually killing off two birds with one stone.

Vivian would never approve of the methods he's used, sending Sara and others to bed with those abominations, but these were sacrifices Chris was willing to make. Sometimes the only way to catch a demon is to become just as devilish as your prey. After everything he has lost, Chris is willing to walk through Hell itself to get what he wants.

If befriending his enemy is the only means to his end, Chris will deal with the devil himself if it gets him one step closer to finding the pack of dogs that stole his wife. The memories come uninvited, and the decades have done little to settle the rage Chris has felt every moment since the Santiago pride helped to rip his world apart.

"Chris, are you home?" Melanie calls from downstairs.

"Yeah, I'm in the office. You need something?" Chris answers, finishing the final details of the finance reports. Being the head accountant for the Human Council demands that he works long hours, as they have a multitude of businesses that donate to the cause.

"Hey, we need to talk," Melanie states from the office doorway.

That statement in itself grabs Chris's attention. Almost no pleasant conversation in the history of the spoken word has ever begun with that opener.

"Chris, I met someone, and I am going to live with him," Melanie confesses nervously.

"You've met someone? When? Who? This is all I get; you are not even willing to try to save our marriage? And what the Hell about Sara? Is that what you plan on telling her, that you found someone?" Chris yells as he flings the files from his desk onto the floor.

Melanie wraps her arms around her body tightly as she watches him. It's only when she steps closer towards him that Chris sees the marks on her neck. Before he thinks about the consequences, he is on his feet, snatching Melanie by the arm to get a closer look at her shoulder.

"What have you done, Melanie? What have those animals done to you?" Chris asks as an enraged shifter races up his stairs. He pulls his wife behind him, ready for a fight to the death with whatever comes through that door.

"You brought this monster to our home?" Chris bellows as this half-mutated beast crashes into his office.

"Get your hands off my mate!" the dog growls out. Everything about this thing screams danger, although Chris can tell that this is just a Beta wolf. One that he can easily dispose of, if he can just get to his weapons safe.

"Don't even think about it," growls another voice. Chris watches in horror as another half-mutated beast comes through the door, this one's eyes glowed Alpha red.

"Do you filthy abominations have any idea who I am? I am Christian Mitchel, seated member of the Human Council. How dare you come into my house, after this fucking dog bit MY WIFE!"

"Chris, I'm sorry! I never meant to hurt you, but I wanted him to bite me! I consented. I just came here to get

Sara!" *Melanie sobs as she cries uncontrollably, clinging to the shifter that had returned to his human form.*

"You wanted to be with this animal? This child? What about Sara? You won't be taking her anywhere!" Chris asserts, as Melanie jumps in.

"I'm her mother! She belongs with me."

Chris sneers at this thing that used to be his wife. "No, you are the whore that abandoned her child to lie with dogs. She won't be going anywhere."

"You can say what you want about me, but DO NOT disrespect my mate again or I will..." the younger shifter warns as he takes a step towards Chris.

Chris bristles. "You will do what, mutt? You are the ones that broke the human/shifter treaty by mate biting a married human. It is well within my rights to seek recompense for this crime," he all but yells as he steps forward; he will not be intimidated in his own home.

"Yes, I know who you are, and you are correct, Mr. Mitchel. As the Alpha, it is my duty to make sure everyone in the pack obeys the treaty. I contacted the Alpha Apex enroute and he has contacted the Human Council. They will be arriving shortly, which is why I am in your home,"

*the Alpha shifter stresses as he moves between Chris and
the younger shifter.*

*Chris nods his understanding. He knows that he is
absolutely justified in his fury and the Council will surely
allow him the satisfaction of killing the man that has tried
to destroy his family.*

Chris/Hugh ~ Present

"So how long after I hit the detonator do I have to get clear of the blast?" the shifter asks, pulling Chis back into the present.

"What's wrong? Scared to singe something that won't grow back?" Chris answers dismissively. He can't help but taunt this animal a little, like a dog on a chair.

"You'll have a little over three minutes to be clear of the blast area, although I wouldn't suggest you dally too long. Never can tell if the cord is going to burn too quick."

"Okay. So, Chris, how is it that you know Sara?" Hugh asks as he watches Chris begin to assemble all the pieces together in the gym bag.

"Well, that would be more information than you need to complete your task."

"Not really, since she is asking me to trust you with my life," Hugh argues.

"Have you asked her?"

"No. I am asking you. So how is it that you know Sara?" Hugh questions. Chris chuckles when he sees the shifter's eyes flash in irritation. He figures no harm can come from this one knowing their connection.

"I am her father. Is that a sufficient enough connection for you?"

"Her father?"

"Yes, so as you can see, I am also trusting you with my daughter's life. So don't fuck this up," Chris adds as he hands the shifter the bag.

Chris watches as the shifter nervously grabs the bag. He is holding it so far away from his body that he will draw too much attention before he even reaches his car.

"It's not going to fucking explode until you detonate it, but if you keep acting like there is a bomb in your bag, you will never make it out of the harbor."

"Fine." The shifter growls, swinging the bag over his shoulder before storming away.

Chapter 5

February 3, 12 p.m.

"Sean! It's so good to see you. You are getting so huge! Here, let me see if I can make you more comfortable," Rebecca says teasingly. Her hands glow slightly as she reaches for him, and Sean can feel the cubs calm.

Sean laughs as his mother strokes his belly with awe. "Thank you, mother dearest. At least I can count on your brutal honesty. Everyone around here is always telling me how wonderful I look. Even though I look like I ate a whale and haven't seen my feet in weeks."

"You do look wonderful; most humans are completely bedridden by this point in their pregnancy. I think it is your magic that is helping you to carry the triplets so well," Tien offers unhelpfully.

"Well, my back doesn't seem to think I'm carrying well," Sean jokes as he rubs his back. The cubs are getting active enough that their movements can be seen on the outside. But that is nothing compared to the feeling of multiple feet and hands knocking into his organs. Some days it's enough to bring him to his knees.

Honestly, Sean often wonders how he is still able to get around so well. It seems like the babies and his belly are growing every day. So the thought that magic is giving him a boost isn't as out there as he would have once thought. Why couldn't it stop him from puking every five minutes and crying like some emotional trainwreck? That would be a magic trick he could get behind.

"So, Mom, I'm guessing it isn't just a case of you dying to get in touch with nature that made you insist that we had to meet out on the edge of the pride lands? Even though I've enjoyed the picnic, I'm sure there is more to it."

"No it isn't, smartass. This is actually the center of the pride land once you include the land I gave to you," Rebecca replies.

"You owned this land?" Tien asks, laughing when Rebecca nods her head in confirmation.

"What's so funny?" Sean asks.

"This is perfect. Richard and DeMatteo have been going crazy for years trying to get the company that owned this property to sell. But they wouldn't budge, and Richard was willing to offer a few million over the value just to get it. It seemed strange that no one ever stepped foot on the land but refused to sell."

"That is quite amusing. To think, had my visions shown me that DeMatteo was Sean's mate, I would have given it to the pride. But our magic is tied to this earth, his more than mine since he is more magic than a simple witch." Rebecca laughs, seems as the fates had been working overtime ensuring Sean and DeMatteo's mating.

"Mom, you never have explained exactly what I am. Just the other day I transported to another room because DeMatteo pissed me off. I need to know what I am capable of before I accidentally blow up my mate," Sean says and there is so much truth to that statement Rebecca shudders thinking about how badly things could go if Sean loses control of his powers.

"Yes, and I'm sorry, but with everything that has happened, I didn't want to overwhelm you. But now with the birth of the babies so near, you need to fully connect to the land of our ancestors. Tien, can you give me a hand? Sean, you are so much more than a simple witch like me. When we are done here, there will be no limits to the magic you can harness. I am limited to spells and rituals; my magic comes from my belief that the Goddess will answer my prayers. The larger my coven, the more faith I can draw upon," Rebecca explains.

"Sean, step inside the circle," Tien commands, her voice a deep rumble as her polar bear rests just beneath the surface. It's almost as if Sean can see it peering out at him, and his lioness's response is immediate, rising up in greeting.

"Tien is a guardian shifter. Her magic is tied to her pride, and she calls on the magic that allows them to change forms to power her intentions. Even though being connected to the entire North American shifters gives her one hell of a power boost, she still has her limits."

"Great Goddess, creator of the earth and all that inhabits it, I call upon you to seal this circle cast in your honor."

"But you, my son, are connected directly to the Goddess and the land. Your will is hers and as long as there is an earth to call upon, your magic is without end. You do not have to bend to the laws of nature. You are the creator of law. Once you have connected with the Goddess you will not need any spells or charms to call upon her."

"This circle is cast and protected by the Goddess. Let no one enter here." Tien continues to speak as the ground around them glows a magnificent blue. Sean watches as Tien uses a powder to draw on the ground.

"That is a Triquetra. It is one of the most powerful symbols in magic," Rebecca explains.

"Is that why you added it to my tattoo?" Sean asks.

Tien nods. "Yes, and now we will be invoking the power of the Triquetra to fully unlock the powers that your mother binded."

"I thought you already did that, Mom, before I mated."

"We did, or we unlocked as much as we could. As I said, Sean, I am merely a witch, so even with the coven I did not possess enough magic to fully unleash yours," Rebecca answers while Tien places and lights the candles and incense on each corner of the Triquetra.

"Okay, Sean, are you ready?" Tien asks.

"I guess so?" Sean answers nervously.

"Don't guess, Sean. Be sure. We will need all your faith for this to work," Tien insists.

Sean takes a deep breath. So much has happened already, but yet it seems as if they are preparing him to take on even more. The triplets choose that moment to kick, and Sean takes it as their approval.

Sean knows he will do whatever it takes to keep his cubs and his mate safe. And this might be the best chance he has at protecting them; his magic has already saved both him and his children. Now that he knows that what he's had is just a portion of what he can be, Sean doesn't hesitate in his answer.

"I'm ready," Sean answers, and he is. He is sure on a level that he has never been about anything in his life. The magic hums in the air, dancing over his skin, so much that his cubs seem to be almost dancing.

"Sean, you must speak these words as we chant and lend you our magic," Tien orders as she hands Sean a piece of paper.

He reads it over twice, committing the simple spell to memory before speaking the words. He can't help but notice that everything around them is unnaturally silent as if everything is collectively holding their breath.

"Powers of high, listen to my plea. Three aspects of the Divine I invoke thee." He begins, and immediately Sean can feel his lioness rise up. Even the babies inside him still as his mother and Tien begin to chant in a language he doesn't understand.

But with each verse, Sean can feel, what he can only guess is, his magic swirl around him. The circle itself seems to reverberate as the power swells and grows inside.

"This magic time, this magic hour, I ask you to return my powers. Bless this symbol with your love. Bless this symbol with your might. I feel you with me day and night," Sean continues.

The winds pick up around them as Tien and his mother's chants reach a fevered pitch. The air feels like it is not just around him but moving through him, and Sean can feel heat as it burns brighter, stoked by the winds.

"Hear my call, hear my plea. Three as One always with me! Three as One forever be!" Sean's vision flips to a reddish hue as flames race through him. He doubles over, clutching his belly as the pain intensifies, dropping him to his knees while his lioness roars.

The waves of magic that had been swirling and growing suddenly slam into Sean, ripping an earsplitting roar from him that can surely be heard for miles. The change happens so suddenly that the stretching of bone and muscle doesn't have time to register before Sean is dragging himself up on all fours.

"Sean!" Rebecca screams, just as the magic explodes and the deafening sound of Sean's roar forces her to cover her ears.

A wave of magic flings her across the field. She has never felt that amount of power come from a single person. Tien is crawling, trying to get back to her feet, but the force of Sean's magic keeps her on her knees. When the ringing finally dies down, Rebecca can see that her baby has shifted into an enormous lion.

Climbing to her feet, Rebecca is unsure if it is safe to approach him. Sean had told her what his lion looked like, but until now Rebecca really had no frame of reference to coincide with the description he had given her.

This lion must weigh a thousand pounds and stands over seven feet tall. His fur is magnificent, with his large flowing mane. She is startled when Tien touches her arm.

Turning, Rebecca is surprised to discover that the other woman is also partially shifted into some strange combination of woman and bear. The hand that grips her arm has claws the size of kitchen knives.

"Just give him a minute. His lion needs to adjust to its new power," Tien lisps out around her fangs.

Sean scents the air. Everything is just more now; his mind is sharp but different. He knows that he is not the same man who stepped into this clearing. Everything is new, the intensity of the sounds, sights, smells, just everything, and it takes him a second to zone in on the two women staring at him.

Sean's fur bristles with power as he studies them. He knows on a primal level that they are his pride. They are his to protect.

"Sean?" Rebecca calls tentatively, palm outstretched towards her son.

Chuffing out a greeting, Sean stretches as his pride mates come closer. Something niggles in the back of his mind as the taller of the two approaches him; there is something familiar about her.

Tien walks up closely, tilting her head in submission. Sean breathes in deep, taking in more of their scents. He meets her halfway, and when she brushes her hands through his mane their connection is immediately forged.

Both the lioness and man are comforted by the lack of fear on the other two, purring low in his chest in acceptance of the other shifter and human's submission. As soon as the human's hand is within distance, Sean runs his rough tongue on the offered hand, causing the human to laugh out loud.

Mother, his lioness acknowledges, as waves of memories flood both of their minds.

"Oh my Goddess, baby, look at you. You are magnificent!" his mother breathes, her voice like a soothing melody running through both him and his lioness.

The tender moment is fractured when a thunderous roar rocks the trees, and Sean's lioness braces in front of her pride mates, readying for an attack.

DeMatteo ~

DeMatteo and Samantha are going through the security feeds from the house when he feels his mate's pain through their bond. He panics for a second before a blaze of electricity shoots through him, forcing him to shift.

"DeMatteo?" He hears his sister call to him, but he is already running the instant his paws hit the ground, the thoughts of *not again* pushing him to move faster. Leaping from the balcony, gasps and screams from others milling around fade into the background as he rushes past them.

DeMatteo's roar is bloodthirsty when the scent of Sean's magic and fear waft past him. He picks up more speed, his nightmares springing to life in his mind. DeMatteo enters into the familiar clearing, past the shack that once held his near lifeless mate's body, when Sean's warning call booms out a challenge, causing his steps to falter.

DeMatteo slows slightly as he begins to feel his mate's presence, warning bells ringing in his ears when he first catches sight of his mate. Sean is fully shifted, crouched low, but even in this position he easily looks to now match DeMatteo's size.

DeMatteo slows further, cautious. Whatever spell work they had been practicing seems to have Sean confused, and his mate rumbles low in warning.

Sean's stare is unwavering as he approaches. DeMatteo begins to push on their bond, hoping to snap his mate out of whatever trance he seems to be trapped in. Sean's growling stops for a moment, while his ears flick and he scents the air. Eons seem to pass before Sean's eyes flash bright orange with him prowling forward, his growls turning into a deep chuffing sound.

DeMatteo holds his ground as Sean presses closer, his nostrils flaring as he continues to test the air. It's almost as if he doesn't recognize DeMatteo. Once they make contact, everything changes.

DeMatteo feels as he is being burned from the inside out. Power races through him, unlike anything he has ever felt before, and he barely notices when his legs fail him.

When he finally comes to, DeMatteo is back in human form, Sean's body tucked safely beside him. DeMatteo startles when he hears his aunt speak, his fangs and claws sliding out quickly to protect his vulnerable mate.

"Welcome back." Tien chuckles brightly. Sean shifts in his arms as DeMatteo struggles to turn towards the voice.

"What happened?" DeMatteo asks.

"Sean received his full powers, and then he transferred some to you," Tien answers.

Sean stretches, eyes fluttering, and DeMatteo is transfixed on the new signs and symbols that are etched into his skin. "And these?" DeMatteo asks distractedly, pointing to the tattoos.

"I'm not sure. They appeared when he shifted back; my best guess is that the Goddess decided to mark him."

DeMatteo turns back only to find Sean's eyes open, watching him carefully. His heart lurches at the tenderness in Sean's eyes. So many things have happened, and through it all, this man's love never seems to waver. DeMatteo doesn't know why the gods have chosen to bless him, but he knows he will spend his last breath trying to be the man that deserves it.

"Holy shit, it feels like I'm connected to a battery," Sean babbles as he struggles to sit up.

DeMatteo slides his arms around Sean, taking his weight easily as his mate changes positions. The cubs are growing daily, and DeMatteo feels nothing but smug as he watches his mate's belly swell more by the day. There is an audible pop as what must have been a protective shield dissipates around them.

"What was that?" Sean asks.

"Tien can create protection circles," DeMatteo answers, standing and helping Sean to his feet.

"Yes I can, but that was all Sean. Neither one of us could come close to you while you were out. It was more powerful than anything I've ever seen," Tien states in awe. Rebecca is nodding in agreement as she stands behind her son.

"What?" DeMatteo asks. He is shocked. Tien has always been the most powerful magic user, but now the way she is staring at Sean makes DeMatteo wonder if just maybe there is actually something to the prophecy.

"It was amazing. The minute you two touched, you were surrounded by light that actually pushed us back. I couldn't see much, but when it was over you were back to human, I tried to check to see if you were okay, but I couldn't get within five feet," Rebecca adds.

"Okay. Not that this isn't amazing, because trust me, I am going to want to discuss this at length, but can we maybe do this back at the house? Because I seem to have ruined my clothes and yeah, I am not that big on being one with nature," Sean chokes out as he tries to hide his dick from his mother and aunt.

Shifters might be comfortable walking around in nothing but a smile, but Sean is human (or mostly human), and the thought of his dick swinging in front of his mother has his face flaming in embarrassment. Sean shoots his mate a glare when he hears DeMatteo stifling his laugh; obviously he is broadcasting his discomfort.

"Sean's right, we should get back before the weather turns cold, I'd hate for DeMatteo to have to carry me back in the rain," Rebecca concedes, grabbing Sean's attention. Looking up, he notices that storm clouds have rolled in, covering what had been a bright sky.

"That often happens when we use powerful magic. It changes the environment around us," Tien offers.

"Ladies, after you," DeMatteo offers. Sean stands back with DeMatteo as his mother and Tien head back towards the pride house. His clothes are in shreds on the ground; there isn't even a piece big enough to tie around his waist.

"You know there is nothing wrong with you being naked." DeMatteo leers as he grabs what's left of Sean's sneakers.

"Yeah, I'm not shy, but my mom is right here," Sean whispers as they start off behind the women. Just thinking about his mom seeing him, and oh my god DeMatteo naked, has Sean's face growing hotter with every step.

"She's your mother. She has seen you naked before," DeMatteo huffs out, obviously amused by his distress.

"Yes but I was… Everything was smaller back then. I was smaller!" Sean insists.

DeMatteo barks out a laugh so Sean elbows him in the gut, hard. They walk the rest of the way in silence, DeMatteo rubbing his stomach and grumbling under his breath the whole way.

Their shower is rushed because Sean is anxious to find out more of the prophecy, but DeMatteo just wants to keep them here, safe inside their den. His lion agrees heartily with the sentiment but there is no way Sean would settle for being hid away like a "damsel in distress," so DeMatteo takes comfort in drying his mate.

It starts off innocently enough, with him taking his time to worship every inch of skin on display. After he is dry, they return to their room to dress. This has become one of the Alpha's favorite rituals. It was calming for both him and his lion and a way for DeMatteo to reaffirm and strengthen their bond through touch.

Reaching for the lotion, DeMatteo pours out a generous amount and begins at Sean's shoulders. He follows the new curves and contours of his mate's ever-changing body, being sure to moisturize every bit of skin. Sean's breath hitches when he reaches his nipples; fascinated with the response, DeMatteo flicks the nub gently just to watch it pebble.

"DeMatteo." Sean growls in warning, though his spike in arousal says something entirely different.

"Yes?" DeMatteo asks, all while giving the other nipple the same treatment.

"We need to get ready," Sean answers breathlessly.

DeMatteo chooses to ignore that statement, pouring more lotion in his palm and kneeling to lotion Sean's belly. The babies kick at his hands as he lazily circles the large bump. He bends to place a kiss on Sean's barely-there belly button, earning a giggle from his mate.

"Turn around," DeMatteo husks. Sean's heartbeat speeds up as he turns around so DeMatteo can focus on his backside. He nips at one round cheek before starting the process, just to enjoy the way Sean's body trembles in response.

DeMatteo spends a few minutes petting Sean's hole, rubbing gently around the rim when Sean spreads his legs a little. Each swipe causes the muscle to wink, opening slightly before closing back tight.

Slick starts to leak around his fingers, so he spreads Sean's cheeks further just to watch it gape and leak some more. DeMatteo carefully licks his fingers clean before pouring more lotion to continue his task.

Once DeMatteo reaches the bottom of his calves, Sean automatically turns for the process to repeat on his lower half. He is not surprised by the erection that nearly smacks him in the face with the motion; that too is part of their ritual.

It's instinct, so he doesn't even have to consider it before he takes Sean's cock into his mouth, moaning as the taste bursts across his senses. Sean's hands immediately slide into his hair, as he pushes his hips forward.

"You have got to be kidding, right? You do realize that my mother and your aunt are downstairs waiting for us?" Sean groans as he pulls back, lust burns brightly as he watches his spit covered erection slide out of his mate's mouth.

DeMatteo slides his hands up, his finger unerringly finding Sean's hole. He slides two in immediately, Sean accepting him easily as the slick squelches around the digits. If it wasn't for the amazing pleasure, Sean would be embarrassed by how eager his body responds to the Alpha.

"I know," DeMatteo states, his clever fingers never missing a beat, before he sucks Sean's cock back into his mouth.

"Ah... Jesus, fuck, DeMatteo!" Sean moans when DeMatteo curves his finger to press on his prostate.

DeMatteo's fingers are not thrusting at all, just keeping a constant pressure, rubbing relentlessly on his prostate. Sean is going to come embarrassingly quick. Sean is leaking heavily now, his inner thighs drenched in the lubrication his body now readily makes.

The scent of his slick is thick and sweet, and the fact that most of the house is filled with shifters that can undoubtedly smell exactly how excited the Alpha makes him sends a bolt of arousal mixed with embarrassment through his system.

DeMatteo pops off his dick with a loud pop before starting to fuck into his ass hard. The sounds of his body sucking in those digits make Sean flush hotter. Sean moans louder, the slick sound of DeMatteo's fingers sliding in and out of his ass make his balls draw up tight.

Sean feels soaked as an embarrassing amount of slick slides out of him even as his cock starts leaking and his balls tighten. He wants to make it last, to ride those fingers forever, but it's all over when his mate speaks and his voice is raw from taking his dick.

"Come on, Sean, give it up. I want you to come with my fingers inside you," DeMatteo demands as he slides in a third finger.

Sean can only moan and writhe as DeMatteo spreads his fingers, opening him wide. Hopefully that is enough of an answer because the ability to form syllables seems to be a lost art at the moment. DeMatteo's chuckle assures him that the message has been received as he dips his head lower to slide his tongue in with his fingers.

Sean fucks back onto DeMatteo's tongue, letting out pathetic little whimpers, but he can't bother to care because his balls are tightening as the familiar heat curls low, making his muscles spasm wildly around the intrusions.

DeMatteo pulls his face away, but before Sean can demand that he get back in there, his tongue is replaced by a fourth finger, and his cock is swallowed to the hilt. That's it; Sean's spine locks as his orgasm is ripped from his balls. DeMatteo takes the opportunity to push in harder, rubbing his prostate mercilessly, prolonging his orgasm.

DeMatteo continues to swallow around him, refusing to lose a drop, until he is whimpering with overstimulation. His limbs are still shaking when he feels his softened cock slipping from the warm recess of DeMatteo's mouth.

Another whimper escapes as DeMatteo gently removes his fingers. Sean can feel their bond glowing in his mind as his lioness rolls and purrs in satisfaction with their mating.

DeMatteo's cock throbs painfully in his boxers as he swallows everything Sean has to give him, but this is all about Sean; his needs can wait. He takes his time kissing, licking, and nibbling his way up, stopping to pay attention to Sean's sensitive nipples.

DeMatteo hovers over Sean, careful of their cubs, nipping his way up his neck to his chin, and just like that they are kissing.

It starts off languid, just loving presses of lips, but ratchets up quickly to him hungrily nipping at his mate's lips, begging for entrance. Sean opens with a groan, and DeMatteo eagerly takes control, grabbing Sean's face in one hand and gripping his hair tightly with the other.

He starts tongue fucking his mouth in a lewd approximation of what he wants to do with his cock, and Sean understands completely as he bites down on DeMatteo's lip hard.

"I want you to fuck my face," Sean states once he sucks in enough air.

DeMatteo freezes, his hips bucking involuntarily at the dirty as fuck suggestion coming from his mate. His first answer is *yesyesyesyes*, but with Sean so far along he can't risk injuring him or the cubs.

Sean must mistake his hesitation for unwillingness as the pungent scent of rejection starts to fill the air as he backtracks.

"Um... unless you don't?" Sean stammers out unsure.

DeMatteo kisses away the hesitation, sending his want and lust for his mate through their bond. "I want. God, baby, you don't even know how much I want, but the babies?" DeMatteo says when he pulls away, making sure to push his aching erection against Sean's leg in case his mate needs further proof of his eagerness.

"Then do it," Sean challenges, before lying on his back.

Never able to deny him anything, and really why would he turn down having his mate's lips wrapped around his dick. DeMatteo carefully climbs over his mate, knees resting on either side of his shoulders, pinning him to their bed.

"Tell me if it's too much? Tap me, fuck, bite my dick, but let me know if you want to stop," DeMatteo pleads. Sean leans his head up to suck on the tip before lying back.

"Yes. I trust you, DeMatteo. You would never hurt me," Sean says before leaning up again. This time he goes for it, hollowing his cheeks and sucking, bobbing his head quickly.

"Oh god," DeMatteo moans as he watches Sean suck his dick.

His eyes almost cross as Sean ups his game, tongue twirling and tracing the thick vein, before easing off to suckle at the tip. Tongue pointed, darting in and out of his piss hole, as if he is trying to get every bead of pre-come before it even leaks.

He fights not to buck into Sean's mouth, regardless of what he said, DeMatteo knows he is quite capable of hurting both his mate and his cubs should he get over excited. He can already feel his control slipping as his fingers tingle and his gums itch, the lion clawing in his brain, all too willing to take what their mate is offering.

"DeMatteo, please. I want it, just let go."

"Sean, I." Every argument DeMatteo was about to offer evaporates when Sean flashes his eyes brilliant orange; he actually whimpers when he notices the flash of fang and the ten claws he can feel pulling on his ass.

"No! I want it. You couldn't hurt me if you tried," Sean rebuts.

The fangs are gone, but DeMatteo can still feel where very unhuman claws threaten to break the skin, and that is what finally breaks his resolve.

Without preamble DeMatteo grips Sean by the hair, yanking him onto his cock. He doesn't ease up until he hits the back of his throat, causing Sean to gag slightly. DeMatteo ignores the sound and just shoves back in, shoving deeper when Sean moans around his length.

"There, now take it," DeMatteo growls in between thrusts.

DeMatteo opens their bond, hoping that this will help him keep his mate's wellbeing in mind, as the lust he feels projected forces him to pull back and wait to catch his mate's eyes before using his hair to shove him down on his cock, hard.

"So beautiful, baby, suck it, baby, just like that," DeMatteo encourages.

Sean whimpers as DeMatteo holds his head still so he can fuck in rough and fast until Sean has to abandon trying to suck and just opens his mouth wider. DeMatteo growls low in his throat when Sean relaxes and just opens; pushing further down, blocking his ability to breathe. Sean squirms so DeMatteo tightens his knees, not allowing him any room to move as he is used.

"You are such a perfect cocksucker, aren't you?" DeMatteo asks absentmindedly, not that he was expecting a response with his cock buried in the other man's throat.

DeMatteo finally loses it when Sean swallows around him reflexively, taking him in more, the first few spurts going straight down his mate's throat. DeMatteo pulls back slightly, allowing Sean to suck in a desperate breath through his nose as DeMatteo continues to flood his mouth.

Sean splutters and chokes slightly and tries to swallow, but DeMatteo is still coming, watching as he pulls further back to paint his mate's face. He strokes himself greedily, as the last drops land on Sean's lips. He wastes no time lying beside his panting mate and licking his face clean.

Once he has lapped up every drop. DeMatteo holds the last remnants on his tongue. Holding Sean still, DeMatteo kisses him, making sure to feed Sean some of his cum off his tongue. Sean responds immediately, desperately sucking on his tongue for every trace, making a distressed sound when there is nothing left of it to be had.

Pulling away, DeMatteo takes in Sean's appearance. His cheeks are flushed and his hair is standing on end from both their hands; he has never been more beautiful. They both sit back enjoying their orgasmic high, but all too soon Sean rolls to his side.

"We really need to get downstairs," Sean says, and DeMatteo can't resist kissing him again.

"I don't want to move; we can always tell them you were sick again," DeMatteo suggests hopefully. Sean laughs, climbing out of bed with more grace than someone would think a man his size could.

"No, my mother and your aunt are waiting, and we've been gone too long as it is," Sean answers, grabbing his clothing.

"Okay, but we need to shower again and brush our teeth," DeMatteo says.

"DeMatteo, we don't…"

"Unless you want us to go downstairs reeking of semen. In front of a shifter and your mother?" DeMatteo cuts in, laughing as Sean's face flushes red with the thought of the others smelling what they've been up to.

"We'll shower together. Behave," Sean announces as he stomps towards the bathroom.

"Uncle Richard? I wasn't expecting you," DeMatteo says as they walk into the main living room. Sean nearly trips over his feet as he notices the older Alpha. DeMatteo tightens his grip on his mate, grimacing at the scent of embarrassment coming from him.

Richard stands, apparently unaware of how uncomfortable the Alpha Mate has become and jokes, "Yes, I just got here a few minutes ago, but you were... Busy." Richard leers, wagging his eyebrows ridiculously at DeMatteo.

Tien clears her throat loudly, smiling when everyone turns to her, before trying to steer the conversation. "If you're done embarrassing Sean, I'd like to discuss the prophecy and how we plan to move forward from here," Tien states, looking pointedly at her mate. Richard has the decency to look properly chastised as he takes a seat beside his mate.

Richard waits until everyone is seated before beginning.

"The prophecy speaks of the time when shifters will be united by one and brought back into the services of the Goddess. It says that these times will begin with the birth of a great Alpha Guardian and that Guardian will mate with a great Alpha in the new world. Once they have come together, their offspring will gather all the shifters and give rise to all those clans that have fallen, uniting both human and shifters and returning us to our rightful place," Richard says before motioning for Tien to continue.

"There's been many different interpretations over the years. The one thing we have always known is that the Alpha would come from the Santiago line. Even though this prophecy was written generations ago, many magic users, including myself and your mother, still have visions. In my visions, I have always seen the Santiago pride standing with the Guardian. When you were born, I had a vision of the Alpha Guardian rising and started making preparations, announcing your arrival to all the Councils. We were connected. I could feel your magic, and I knew it was the one of the legend. Then one day you disappeared," Tien says.

"I bound your magic to protect you. I also had visions that showed you as a leader of men, but one night the Goddess came to me and told me that you were in great danger. There are many who fear what the prophecy can mean, and they wanted to destroy you before you could come fully into your power. The Goddess told me to protect you above all else, so the coven sealed your magic away, hoping that whoever sensed you would lose track of you without it. It worked for a time, but then I died," Rebecca says sadly.

"That is unfortunately what has brought me out here today," Richard interrupts. The look on his face is enough to put Sean on alert; he seems nervous and irritated, and that can't be a sign of anything pleasant.

"What?" Sean asks.

"Rebecca's albeit temporary death and subsequent resurrection. It now looks like it might not have been the tragic accident that we had all assumed."

"What are you talking about? My former body was killed in an accident. It was just a little girl. I've seen the reports. She was barely older than you were at the time, and she had taken her parents' car and lost control and…" Rebecca states frantically.

"Yes, but there is more. The Human Council knew the child that was in the vehicle. They feared your coven would seek retribution on the child of a hunter. So they hid her, used a false name to the police and made sure no evidence connecting her to your death was left. They believed that she hit you intentionally, that she knew you were a witch and went out that day to kill you, and succeeded."

"How do you know this? If they've hid it all these years, why admit it now?" Sean asks.

"Reynold called me this morning to inform me. The Human Council held a vote and decided that they needed full disclosure because of everything that has happened to you and DeMatteo. The little girl that ran you over was Sara Mitchel, and they believe she knew exactly what she was doing."

"What!" Rebecca shouts at the same time Sean says, "Oh, god, I'm gonna be sick." He doesn't make it to his feet before emptying his stomach, but DeMatteo catches him as he sways dangerously.

"I am going to kill her," DeMatteo growls, sweeping Sean up bridal style and carrying him out of the room.

Tien ~

"Not if I find her first," Rebecca adds coolly. The look in her eyes leads Tien to believe that this little witch might be more dangerous than she appears. Tien waits until Sean and DeMatteo have left hearing range before addressing the witch.

She watches as the human paces; Tien can feel the magic that is pulling up around the woman. It's much weaker than her own, but almost black with anger, and it doesn't take much to sense what the human is feeling.

"I know you want vengeance for the life this woman stole from you, but I must caution you to not interfere. If we are indeed living in the times of the prophecy, it is paramount that we allow the Alpha Pair to reach their full potential," Tien speaks quietly.

"I understand the prophecy! I have spent my entire life preparing for and protecting Sean, but if you think I am going to sit back and watch as the woman who tried to kill me, seduced my son, and tried to kill him and my grandchildren tries to make another mistake you are sorely mistaken. I might not be a shapeshifter like the others or a powerful mage like my son, but I am far from harmless."

Tien nods her head in easy acceptance; this human, while weaker, is no doubt a dangerous woman. Tien can't begin to imagine how it feels to know this woman has attacked every part of her family, but the prophecy must come first, and for that Sean will need to face and defeat his enemies.

"I agree, and I am sure you still have a vital role to play yet. But for now we must wait until the hunters make their move. We need to see how many people are against us. For now, I am asking you to trust us to keep your son safe. You know DeMatteo would die before he let anyone close to his mate and cubs." Tien can see anger and fear in every line of the human's body as she comes to a stand in front of the massive windows looking out into the yard. The seconds drag on in complete silence, and Tien and Richard watch Rebecca breathe in deeply before speaking.

"I will trust you and my son, for now. Don't make me regret it." It's a tenuous agreement at best, but Tien doubts that anyone could expect the mother to concede any more.

Chapter 6

"Heaven has no rage like love to hatred turned /
Nor hell a fury like a woman scorned." ~ William
Congreve

The flight from New York to Idaho was uneventful.
It was a calculated risk to fly; shifters seemed to like to
stick their filthy paws into just about everything, but her
documents are bulletproof. That, along with the new scent
blocker her father sent, makes her feel reasonably safe. She
only has her carry-on; the things she needs can't be carried
on any flight, so she heads directly towards long-term
parking.

Chris has arranged for a "clean" car to be waiting
for her at the airport. It's completely legal and tied to the
name she is now using. Sara needs to pick up some
weapons before driving across state lines, stopping at
multiple dealers to not draw too much attention.

They won't be as good as the gear she had to
abandon with Hugh, but she is planning on taking full
advantage of Idaho's lax gun laws. She shouldn't need to
make too much contact with her father; as long as Hugh got
her supplies from Chris, there would be no need for the two
Mitchels to risk being seen together.

Blending into the crowd has long been one of Sara's unique abilities; she could imitate nearly any accent well enough to fool locals. Entering the small gun shop, she notices that the men seem more interested in her cup size than her ID.

"Hello, sweetheart. Looking for something in particular?" the overweight, balding man behind the counter asks.

"Actually, yes. I need two Sig Sauer forty caliber handguns."

"Well, you certainly have good taste. The Sig is one of our most reliable pieces, but a forty caliber round has a lot of punch. You sure you don't want to see one of our more discrete models?"

"Yes, I'm sure. I like big guns," Sara purrs.

"A lady after my own heart," the clerk says as he reaches for the weapons. Sara normally loathes being ogled by men like this, but at this rate she doubts the man would be able to describe anything other than the shape of her ass.

"Thank you. Oh yeah, I'm going to need a few cases of loadable shell casings," Sara adds as the clerk begins to ring up her purchase. In the end, she winds up with an employee discount and Earl's phone number. She waves again before climbing in the car, and she drops the number to the ground before pulling off in the direction of the highway.

She is a few hundred miles down the road before Sara allows her mind to wander off the mission at hand. Even though Chris has explained that her mother was likely killed as soon as the wolves lost interest in torturing her, the fact that they have never found a body leaves the slight chance that Sara could one day find her mother alive.

She tries not to let the thought of her mother still being alive out there somewhere, interfere with her mission. The thought of her being held by those abominations for all these years is worse than the thought of her being dead.

The only thing that brings her any measure of comfort is the thought of finally being able to pay the Santiago pride back in kind. They had refused to help her father save her mother, taking away the one person that Sara loved more than life itself, so she will see to it that DeMatteo loses any and every thing he loves.

Sara ~

"Daddy, where are we going?" Sara asks as Chris straps her in the backseat of her grandparents' van.

"Nana and Poppop found the people that took Mommy, and we are going to get her back, princess," Chris answers as he tucks a blanket around her.

"Really, Daddy?" Sara asks, hugging onto Pebbles, the doll her mother had given her before disappearing. It never left her sight; Sara can still remember being so excited when her mother had showed her the stitching of their initials over the doll's heart.

"Yes, really. Now go back to sleep, sweetie," Chris answers, kissing her on the forehead.

Sara squirms in her seat. Her birthday is coming soon, and there is nothing she wants more than to find her mommy. Last year, shifters had come and stolen her from their home. That day when she got home, Sara had found her house torn apart and her father crying in the kitchen.

That was the day that Sara learned about shifters, and how dangerous they were. Her daddy had made her swear that she would never tell anyone what had happened.

Only special humans knew about shifters, and if others found out, they might kill her mom as punishment.

That was also the day that Sara had learned about her family's secret: they were hunters, some of the special humans who knew the truth about shifters and kept the other humans safe. Later that night, Nana and Poppop had come and Daddy had sent her to her room, but she could still hear pieces of what they said.

The next week when she had finally decided to ask her father what "mates" were, he explained soulmates and that her mom was his, and that is why they stole her. But now they are going to bring her mother back home, and Sara is trying desperately to do as she is told and go back to sleep, but she is too excited.

Sara wakes up again alone in the car, there are sounds of fireworks off in the woods. She knows her father would want her to stay in the car, but she is excited to see them. She climbs out, her favorite doll held tightly to her chest, as she tries to follow the sounds ahead.

Though the noise is deafening, the lights she can see barely break through the thickness of the trees. Sara had nearly given up her search, heading towards the sounds when everything changes; the fireworks have stopped but now she hears animals roaring from every direction.

Sara freezes and tries to look out into the darkness. The sounds seem to be coming from every direction. Although she has never met one, Sara is sure that the sounds she is hearing are shifters. Her father had told her how they could change into savage animals and kill without restraint, and now she is alone in the dark, surrounded.

The panic seems to hold her paralyzed for hours, but then she hears screams of people and that gets her moving again. She turns around to go back to the van, only to slip and fall on the muddy ground. More fireworks light up the night sky as more and more animals join in on the call.

Even her childlike mind pieces together that the shifters are attacking, and they are coming closer. She needs to get back to the car.

"Run!" Sara hears her Nana scream as she scrambles back to her feet. She falls every few steps; the ground is wet and slick, but she has to keep going. She knows if the shifters find her she will be killed.

"Get to the damn van, Chris!" Sara hears her grandfather order as more fireworks explode, much closer than they were before.

"Daddy!" Sara cries as she crawls. She can't find Pebbles.

"Sara? Sara where are you?" Chris screams frantically.

"I'm here, Daddy! I can't find Pebbles!" Sara answers. She is reaching through the mud when she finally feels something, but before she can get a grip, her father snatches her into his arms.

"Daddy!" Sara holds on tight, her tiny body shaking as her father runs towards safety.

"Why would you leave the car? I could have lost you too, don't you understand? These are animals. They would have killed you or worse," Chris explains shakily as he pushes her into the backseat.

There are guns thrown all around, and her grandparents are screaming for them to hurry. They tear away violently, throwing her around, and Sara struggles to pull the seatbelt over her shaking frame.

"Where's Mommy?" Sara asks between tears, although she already knows the answer. When her father doesn't answer, she asks her beloved Nana. "Nana? Where's Mommy?"

"We were too late, baby. They've moved her. And these animals refuse to tell us where," her grandmother answers, and Sara knows she will never see her mother again.

"Nana! I lost my baby." Sara cries harder as she hugs the blanket hastily thrown over her.

Not only did her mother not return, but she's lost the last gift her mother had given her last year, right before her fifth birthday.

Sara ~ Present

The sound of her cell phone forces Sara from the past. Looking at the incoming number, she has to take a deep breath before answering.

"Are you back in town yet?" Hugh asks as soon as Sara answers.

"Not yet. I should be at the address I sent you in a few hours. Were you able to find everything on the list?"

"Yes, even though most of this shit will be useless. There is no way we will get DeMatteo away from the witch long enough to use it." Hugh complains and Sara can't stop from rolling her eyes in contempt.

"No, and even if we did, there is no guarantee it would work. No, this package is for the others helping the witch. If we destroy the people helping him, it might weaken him enough for us to attack him," Sara explains slowly.

It's almost as if she is dealing with an inept child, and it's times like this she wishes she had just put a bullet in his brain and been done with it.

"That seems like a very smart plan. Makes me wonder why you didn't tell me that to begin with," Hugh states, although his tone is accusing.

"Well, I didn't want you to go off half-cocked... again. I really don't have to remind you what happened last time, do I?"

"No, you don't. There were many mistakes made last time, by both of us. I know one of my biggest mistakes was not knowing the entire plan. But this time we are going to work together, aren't we?"

"I'm not sure if I hate this new personality you've developed or not. But I am doing this to help you, Hugh, and suddenly you are acting as if I am the enemy. What happened to the Hugh I met?"

"That little boy is long dead and buried. I've learned a lot from having my mate stolen and being driven from my pride. I've learned that being weak is why some witch was able to walk in and destroy my life. Had I fought harder, he would have never been able to place such a powerful spell on DeMatteo," Hugh growls out, and Sara can just make out the words around the lisp of his fangs.

"You know I understand how you feel. I too lost my mate."

"You have no idea how I feel! You have no idea how my lion feels. Losing your mate may have been hard, but you are human. You can move on. DeMatteo is it for me. My lion will never accept anyone else. So I will do anything, and I mean any fucking thing, to get him back. And I will destroy everything or anyone who gets in my way!" Hugh screams.

"Well then, if that's the case, you shouldn't have any problems doing what you are told this time. You will get your mate, and I'll get to punish Sean for taking mine and killing Nick," Sara concedes. It seems like the shifter is even more unstable than the last time they were together. This can prove to be a problem if she can't get him to fall in line.

Hugh pauses for a few seconds and seems more composed when he adds, "This time we are partners. No more hiding shit from me."

"Deal. Have you finished your first mission?" Sara agrees easily.

"Not yet. I'm headed there right now. Although I still think we should wait for Monday morning."

"I thought of that, but would you really want to risk DeMatteo being there? Anyway, this is just to send a message to Sean."

"Yeah, you're right. This is a better plan. Thank you, Sara, I wasn't sure you'd come back to help."

"Hugh, I told you I'd see this through to the end, and even though you don't seem to always think so, I am your friend."

"Yeah, you're right, and I'm sorry. It's just with everything that's happened, it's hard to keep my head straight sometimes."

"I understand, and after we finish this, I'm sure you'll get what you deserve. You and DeMatteo will be together."

"Yeah. I'm almost there now," Hugh says instead of addressing her comment.

Not wanting to push their fragile alliance Sara decides to let it go. "Okay, Hugh, stay safe. Goodbye."

February 15, 11:30 a.m.

When Sara had first contacted him with her plans, Hugh had almost hung up in her face. But the reality was that he still needed the human's help if he wanted to get his mate back. He wouldn't trust the woman, but she had access to things he could never dream of getting.

This is why he finds himself arriving in the small town of Snohomish at 11:30 a.m. Hugh had never understood why the pride insisted on having most of their businesses in this small town, so far away from the city. But now, Hugh is thankful for their insistence on staying away from large human territories. It was going to make his job much easier.

The streets are deserted where he parks. His target is about a mile away, so Hugh walks at a normal pace. A few cars pass him, and the drivers smile and wave as they go. Hugh's lion paces inside, waiting for the show.

When he gets across from the offices, Hugh lets his lion closer to the surface, his sunglasses hiding his flashing eyes from any human who may see him. He scents the air carefully. It's not likely that DeMatteo would have left that witch to come in on a weekend, but he would never intentionally hurt his mate.

He goes to the front lobby doors and uses the access code he had stolen from DeMatteo a long time ago. Once inside, he heads down to the basement, following the detailed blueprints Chris provided. It takes a few minutes to locate the support beams, but once he does, it's simple to place the bombs on them and attach the cords to the receiver.

Hugh slips back outside and locks the doors. He carefully urinates on the doors, wanting to leave his unmistakable calling card. He needs his mate to know that he has not given up, that he will fight to the end for them to be together.

It takes all his willpower to wait until he is across the street to hit the switch. He just wishes he could see the look on his Alpha's face once he picks up Hugh's scent. Hugh tries not to look back as he heads towards his car. There are more people out on his way back, so Hugh smiles and waves in greeting as he passes.

Hugh is barely behind the wheel when it goes, and the sound is so loud his lion lets out a whine in response. He puts the car in gear heading directly towards the highway, focusing on maintaining his speed to not attract any attention.

By the time he hits the highway, Hugh is completely relaxed. He reaches in the back for the venison he packed for the trip as he heads to his next destination.

Hugh presses the detonator and turns quickly to leave the scene. Although the Hunter Council most likely haven't been informed of the bombing in Snohomish yet, it wouldn't be wise for him to be spotted outside the coven of human witches. It would be suicide if hunters started tracking him; killing humans went against the treaty.

It wouldn't matter that these humans were working with Sean to steal his mate. The hunters would track him down and execute him.

By the time Hugh is back in his car, the predetermined three minutes is winding down; this will finally level the playing field against the witches. Even though more and more humans start down the busy streets, Hugh pauses to witness the explosion.

By the time it reaches the ten-minute mark, Hugh realizes that the second bomb must be a dud. He considers briefly returning to get the bag but quickly dismisses it. He wore gloves the entire time. So unless the witches spot him on the street or hire someone to search for a scent, there will be no trail for them to follow.

Hugh drives cautiously, taking a winding path of side streets until he is safely on the other side of the city before grabbing his cell. He hits his first speed dial and waits. Hugh almost launches his phone out the window when a mechanical voice prompts him to leave his message at the beep.

"Hey, it's me. We have a problem. I'll meet you at the house. Get there as soon as you can," Hugh says.

Chapter 7

February 15, 6 p.m.

"Good evening, Mr. Santiago. My name is Detective Ellis. Thank you for getting here so quickly. Is this one of the firm's partners?" Ellis asks as he looks at Samantha and DeMatteo.

"No, this is my sister, Samantha Santiago. What's happened?" DeMatteo asks, annoyed.

Ellis doesn't answer. Instead, he begins to line up various pictures featuring burnt beams and furniture. It's not until the last photo that shows what is left of his law offices that DeMatteo sucks in a breath.

"That is a very good question, Mr. Santiago. Do you know any reason why someone would want to blow up your law offices?" Ellis asks.

DeMatteo can't take his eyes off the extensive amount of damage in the photos. "Excuse me?" he finally stammers out, eyes snapping up to meet the human's.

"Do you have any idea why someone would intentionally blow up your building?" Ellis repeats, enunciating each word slowly. DeMatteo has to swallow the sudden urge to slam the man's head through the desk.

"Are you sure someone did this? I was told on the phone there had been an accident," DeMatteo says.

"No, this is no accident. Someone used explosives to almost level your law offices, and three people are dead. So you can imagine we have a few questions as to why someone would want to hurt you.," Ellis announces confidently.

"What makes you think the person is after my brother?" Samantha asks, trying to draw away the detective's attention before her brother completely loses it.

"Mrs.?" Ellis begins, looking her over like some piece of meat on display.

"Ms. Santiago," Samantha answers, her lioness growling beneath the surface.

"Thank you. Ms. Santiago, it is a well-known fact that when someone bombs a building, it is either the owner of said building or someone that is looking to send a message to the owner. Either way, it leads to me asking your brother who would risk killing people to send him that kind of message," Ellis questions, it's easy to see that he is certain DeMatteo knows something.

"Is that an actual question?" DeMatteo asks. The accusation is hardly subtle, and while he knows this is how the game is played, it's another thing entirely when it's him under scrutiny.

"That is a question, Mr. Santiago."

"Well, here is your answer: I have no idea why someone would blow up my building. And no, I didn't have anything to do with anyone blowing up my building. So if there are no more questions, is there someone here who can tell me the names of my employees who have lost their lives? I'd like to speak to their families," DeMatteo growls out as he stands. This is about all he is willing to stand from this human.

"Actually, I have a few more questions," Ellis answers, standing and placing himself between DeMatteo and the door.

"Well, unless you plan on arresting me, you can address any further inquiry to my attorney."

"If that is the way you want to play it, Mr. Santiago," Det. Ellis says, reaching for his cuffs. The door opens suddenly as the District Attorney storms into the interrogation room, the Police Captain hot on his heels.

"Mr. Santiago, you are free to go. Thank you for coming in so quickly. Captain Ferguson would be happy to get you the information on your employees. Their families have already been called in to identify the bodies," Dimitri Fleno, District Attorney and leopard shifter says, shaking both DeMatteo and Samantha's hands.

Two detectives follow them down to his building; DeMatteo needs to secure confidential client files. Luckily, they are a pair of shifter cops on duty, so DeMatteo won't have to try to hide the fact that he plans on scenting the area to figure out who did this.

The scent is so strong DeMatteo doesn't need to shift to tell exactly who had set the bomb. His lion growls low in his throat at the betrayal of a once trusted pride mate. To think this is the same man that once shared his bed makes DeMatteo's fangs drop.

"DeMatteo," Samantha says as soon as she picks up the scent.

"Yes, I can smell it too. It's definitely Hugh, although he has to have someone working with him. The man is smart, but no way did he build this bomb on his own," DeMatteo answers as they enter what's left of the building.

The pictures did little to paint the true level of destruction the bomb caused. Looking through the wreckage, DeMatteo knows that if this had been done during a workday, the death count would have been staggering.

"We need to alert the pride that he is back in the area. I want Sean's security detail doubled around the clock. I don't want anyone getting near my mate," he tells Samantha as he carries another box of case files out to his trunk.

"Yes, Alpha. Do you want to take this and head back to the house now?" she asks, carrying another stack of boxes.

He wants to go back to his mate, but DeMatteo has to make sure there will still be a company to run. His clients are worth millions, and if their information gets compromised, it could cost the pride millions in litigation, not to mention DeMatteo losing his license.

"No, just make the calls. I need to check on the families of the victims. Also call Vanessa and tell her we need to make sure these families are taken care of. They have been hurt by a member of the pride, and we must make restitution. I want trust funds set up for any surviving children and their widows."

"Yes, Alpha," Samantha says as she grabs her phone and starts making the calls.

DeMatteo heads back to his offices. The safes will also need to be moved but right now they are safe enough. He will have security guards set up around the clock to make sure no one else comes in to vandalize the property; no way is he trusting this to the local police department.

He is so engrossed in making plans that Samantha startles him and his lion when she speaks.

"DeMatteo, we have another problem," she says, walking in the office. DeMatteo's eyes flash red at the implication.

"Jesus fuck, what now?"

"Uncle Richard just called. There was another bomb."

"You have got to be kidding. Where, and was anybody else hurt?" DeMatteo asks. If Hugh has caused one more death, DeMatteo is going to hunt him down and tear out his throat. DeMatteo can't help but feel responsible for the humans who have already died because he didn't kill Hugh when he had the chance.

"No one was hurt; looks like that one didn't go off."

"Thank the Goddess," DeMatteo says, but then he notices the way Samantha is holding herself rigid; that alone has his lion on alert.

"But there is a bigger problem. This bomb was found at the Hunter Council's main offices. They have some wolves coming to scent the bomb, and I doubt that two different people were out planting bombs tonight."

"Goddammit! Let's go. We need to get ahead of this before the humans send out a hunting party."

This is so much worse than anything DeMatteo could have imagined. If Hugh has attacked the Human Council, then that can be seen as an act of war. If they call in a hunting party on the lion pride, there will be many deaths, both human and shifter. Suddenly this is so much more than a crazy, scorned ex-lover looking for revenge. No, this could be the cause of the next species war.

His lion is all but clawing through his brain; the pride is in danger. DeMatteo grabs his phone as they head back out to the SUV. He needs to reach out to his mate. It's the only thing he knows that can keep his lion under control. DeMatteo can see Samantha watching him carefully as he listens to the phone ring, and he is just about to hang up when the call is finally connected.

"Hello?" comes the sleepy voice of his mate, and that alone is enough to make his lion still inside his mind.

"Hey, baby, it's me. Sorry to wake you," DeMatteo says as Samantha pulls away from the curb. It's about an hour back to his uncle's home, and he can only hope that his uncle is able to keep the humans from declaring a full out war.

"That's fine. I was just taking a nap. Is everything okay?" Sean asks. DeMatteo can feel him gently probing their bond, obviously sensing his distress.

"Sean, it's bad. Hugh is back in town. He blew up my building. Three people are dead, and it looks like he set another bomb at the Human Council."

"Oh my god! What are you going to do?"

"I'm headed over to my uncle's now. I want you to have your security detail take you to his home."

"What? You don't really think he would try to get back on the pride lands, do you?" Sean asks, and DeMatteo wants to smack himself for worrying his mate even more. While he does want to keep his mate safe, he can't pretend that is the main reason he wants Sean with him.

"No it's not that, I just… I'll just feel better having you close to me."

"Alright. I'm on my way." Sean exhales. The tension is still clear in his voice, but DeMatteo can tell his words have given him some measure of comfort.

"Okay see you soon. Love you."

"Love you too," Sean replies before disconnecting the phone. DeMatteo looks at the device in his hands. Hugh has really set a dangerous game in motion. DeMatteo has to find a way to contain him and the hunter female, before other shifters are called in to clean up the mess.

Chapter 8

March 1, 5:30 a.m.

Sara takes her time looking over the hunters her father has sent as backup. Physically they seem to be well trained, but this is a mental game they are waging. Man to man, no human would ever stand a chance against those filthy shifters. No, you have to outthink them, out maneuver them. And those are skills she doesn't have time to teach.

"My father says that you three have been extremely loyal to our family, so I'd like to thank you. I can't imagine it's been easy to stand your ground in a Council with humans who have decided to serve these animals," Sara says to the three hunters.

Chris had been adamant that these men are more than trustworthy. But if there is one thing Sara has learned, it is that loyalty is a subjective term, and the only way to determine a person's worth is to test everyone regardless of who recommends them. It just so happens that she has the perfect test for them. If they fail this step they will be of no use to her in the future.

"Well, I plan on calling them out on their bullshit, but in order to achieve our mission, we will be working closely with a shifter."

"I don't work for abominations," the large redhead says, crossing his massive arms across his chest.

"Is that so?" Sara questions absently as she considers the man.

Most old school hunters balk at the idea of a woman leading them, Sara is under no delusion that at some point she would need to set the tone of their alliance. Big Red smirks as she closes the distance until they are face to face. Easily towering over her, he has clearly dismissed her as no real threat.

The confidence his size gives him is the main reason he fails to notice her petite hands before it's too late. Sara's smile is wide when his eyes bulge comically as he feels the blade press into his groin.

"No, you work for me, and I am telling you that we will be 'working' with a shifter. He doesn't know I am a hunter, so by association he won't know you are either. You will do nothing to raise his suspicion. If you don't think you can do it, I suggest you walk away now and save us all the embarrassment. Because if you accept this job and your macho posturing bullshit fucks up my mission, I will take my time until you are begging for me to end your suffering," Sara warns, never removing the blade from where she has it, digging ever so slightly into his flesh.

"Yes, we understand," Big Red replies, and the others nod their agreements, holding their breaths as if their lives were in peril.

"Good, so now we just have to get you in the right frame of mind," Sara announces cheerily, tapping the tip of her blade absentmindedly.

She makes sure to look each man in the eye, so there would be no misunderstanding that they would pay for any betrayal with their lives. She waits as they each glance down to where she is pressing her knife into the biggest hunter's groin. Once she is satisfied her point has been made, Sara smiles brightly.

"Now, the first rule is that you are to speak as little as possible to the shifter. His name is Hugh; he was part of the pride we're now hunting. He knows nothing about us being hunters, and it will remain that way. You will wear scent blockers and take scent suppressors for the duration. I cannot stress how important this is. There is no way to block strong emotions, but this will hide any subtle shifts in your scent."

"So who are we supposed to be?" Big Red asks.

"What is your name? I can't keep calling you 'Big Red' in my mind. It's distracting," Sara counters.

"Carl?" he answers, although it comes out like more of a question than a statement, but Sara figures she can ignore his indecision. After all, she did pretty much threaten to cut off his dick.

"That's easy, Carl. You are guys that work for me. I'll handle any questions as they come up, and you three will follow my lead," Sara explains, tucking her knife away before asking, "any more questions?"

"No, ma'am!" they all answer in unison.

"Great! So then tell me, are you guys ready to kill some animals?" Sara asks, handing the scent blockers they've had made special for this job. Nodding their agreement each man dry swallows their pill and grabs their gear.

As she heads toward the door, Chris catches her eye. She smiles sweetly at her dad as she leaves the

warehouse, her new team in tow. She needs to grab Hugh
for this next part. Going into a hunter safe house is a ballsy
move, so she will need his senses to get them in and out
safely.

Hugh ~ March 1, 7:30 p.m.

Hugh is watching the news when he hears the lower door open. No one in this building ever has visitors in the middle of the day. Focusing on the sound of four heartbeats as their owners climb the stairs, his lion slips to the surface as Hugh scents the air. He pulls in his fangs and claws, recognizing the scent of Sara and other humans, returning his attention back to his show.

"So you want to go on a little field trip?" Sara asks as she walks into Hugh's apartment.

"Don't you ever knock? And who is that in the hallway?" Hugh asks without looking away from his television.

"Why knock when you can hear me before I even get into the building? And those are guys that are going to help us. I told you this coven has fucked a lot of people over, so it's easy to find others willing to help. But these guys don't know you are a shifter, so it's up to you how much you show them. I told them you are an intelligence specialist and that you can help get us into secure buildings," Sara explains as she whispers low enough that only Hugh can hear.

The hunters already know the plan, but she has to keep Hugh thinking he has some control of the situation. She eyes the television as he watches her silently, going over what she's told him, scenting for any smell of deceit. He doesn't know that she takes pills that render his senses useless when it comes to her emotions.

"That might be for the best. We don't want too many humans knowing about shifters. If we need them when we face the pride, we can tell them then," Hugh concedes.

"So what is this 'field trip'?"

"Ah, right back to business then. I know where some of his coven is meeting, and I want to take them out, cut off his power source," Sara answers.

"And you need me to get you in?"

"Yes, I have no idea what kind of security measures they have, but you can scent if we are walking into some kind of trap."

"Where did you get the information?" Hugh asks before pulling on his jacket. It's obvious he is just fishing for details so Sara relents.

"My dad. He knows a lot of people."

"Ah, so he's not just Chris anymore." Hugh chuckles.

"You know he is my dad. You said you wanted to know everything," Sara says, heading to the door. She has to take a deep breath when she hears him chuckling behind her, and she steadily reminds herself that she can't kill him until later.

Hugh locks the door as they head out. His lion is pacing just below the surface, the scent of the three humans standing near the stairs causing his nostrils to flare. Something about them makes his gums itch, fangs threatening to drop, as he scents their stench of fear and resentment. He notes that the scent of fear spikes as Sara passes them, and Hugh is strangely fascinated by that base reaction.

"So, Sara tells me you need help getting into a building." Hugh aims for small talk as they make their way to their vehicles. He chuckles as all three instantly look to Sara before nodding and mumbling out responses.

"We'll ride together in my vehicle," Sara says as she stops in front of a large SUV.

The windows are heavily tinted, and the sides are marked with some security company's logo. He can smell the same clover scented tobacco that clings to the red haired man, wafting from where he must have sat on their ride over.

"This way we don't have to worry about anyone getting lost if this ends up going to shit," Sara explains before Hugh can level his complaints.

Hugh grunts in response. It makes sense for them to stick together. It could be fatal for anyone to get trapped by a magic user alone. They are way more dangerous than any shifter or regular human. Which is why most other supernaturals try to stay clear of them at any cost; magic is too unpredictable and almost impossible to detect.

Although he can't argue her logic, Hugh adds, mostly to be contrary, "No smoking in the car."

Hugh climbs in the middle row, smiling as the large redhead frowns before heading to the backseat. He notices two rifles tucked under his seat and looks up in time to see Sara smiling at him.

"Tranquilizer rounds," Sara offers. His face must give away his questions because she chuckles as she starts the vehicle. "What? You couldn't have thought that we were going in there with only our good looks?" Sara jokes as she pulls out into traffic. Hugh can't help but smile. He doesn't need a weapon. He is one.

Getting inside is child's play. Hugh hangs back and trains his ears inside as one of the humans works the flimsy locks. He easily makes out four heartbeats on the second floor; catching Sara's eye Hugh holds up four fingers, indicating the number of people inside.

Once the door is open, Sara grabs his arm. "Hugh, once we get inside, I want you to lead, but don't do anything without my say so." Hugh has to bite back a growl at her tone but decides to let it go.

The hallway is barely lit as they make their way towards the witches. Hugh's body is on full alert as he listens, trying to feel any traps they may have set. He can feel his lion rising to the surface, and he is grateful the other humans are protecting the rear as he shifts his eyes. The main entrance and stairways are empty, but Hugh can hear the witches arguing over something as he makes his way through the building.

When they finally make it to the heartbeats, Hugh can hear that the conversation has heated up. There is a large door between them and their prey, and Hugh turns towards Sara lifting a brow as to say "Well, now what?"

"This is where you come in," Sara whispers lower than any human can hear.

Hugh can't hide the smile stretching his lips as he pushes past the humans and kicks in the large wooden door. The witches jump from their seats, but it's already too late; Sara and the other humans are already moving.

Each witch is shot once in the chest before they can utter a word, and Hugh just watches in amazement at the near instantaneous way they all just drop to the ground as the fast acting drug does its job. A peek at his phone says it's just past 9 p.m., and this all has been so childishly easy, Hugh is questioning why he's even here.

Sara ~ *March 1, 10:30 p.m.*

Sara smiles as she watches Reynold's eyes flutter open. She reaches over to remove his gag and he coughs roughly before squaring his shoulders in defiance.

"Sara, you can't seriously believe that you are going to walk away from this," Reynold spits out after he looks around and notices that the others are gagged and tied to chairs facing him.

"Of course I will. Am I really supposed to be afraid of a group of pathetic old men? What are you going to do? Tell me what a bad girl I've been? Send me off to live with Henry so he can reform me?" Sara taunts as she toys with one of her knives.

"Oh well that won't work, seeing as I already killed Henry." Sara looks at Reynold in mock horror as she gasps.

"By the looks on your faces, I can see that you hadn't figured that bit out. Yes, I killed Henry, along with his wife and his darling little babies. It's obvious that you have all seriously misjudged the level of depravity I am willing to wallow in to achieve my goals. But I aim to teach you. Yes, what is left of you will serve as a notice to the others," Sara announces calmly as she slits Maria's throat.

"God! Sara, think about what you're doing!" Stephen yells. Even as a human, Sara can smell the fear that rolls off the older hunter. She wipes the bloodied knife off on Maria's dress before heading over to the others.

"Oh, I've thought about it. As a matter of fact, it's all I've thought about for years," Sara answers, moving beside the older hunter.

She signals for Hugh to restrain him when he resists her putting back in his gag. But she doesn't want him to say anything that might further raise the shifter's suspicion.

"And now it is time that I receive my just repayments." Sara is careful as she slits both of his wrists, letting the blood flow into the bowls she had positioned earlier. She doesn't want to cut too deep; he needs to linger and watch his friends die for his sins.

Sara looks at the other hunters before grabbing the bowls and stepping to the side. "Now is the time you prove your loyalty. Kill them all," Sara orders, leaving Hugh and the three new recruits to take care of the dirty work while she leaves her message for the "Alpha."

Hugh ~

Hugh looks at the humans that are in part responsible for him losing his mate. His lion is rubbing under his skin, demanding the right to kill those who have destroyed his pride. He takes a breath, trying to regain some semblance of control, but the scent of blood from the dead and dying only further agitate the predator.

Hugh springs towards the last two humans. He can distantly hear the three humans that came with him as his lion tears through his body, shredding his clothes in the process. If his mind wasn't so focused on eviscerating the first man, he might have considered their presence before shifting.

But his lion wants blood. Landing on the man, Hugh bites into his shoulder, knocking the chair over onto the floor. Warm blood sprays into his mouth and onto his fur. Hooking his back paws into his prey's belly, Hugh pulls until he is able to pull the limb from the torso and toss it away.

Hugh stops to lap at some of the blood as it pools under the body, but the smell of urine and feces pushes him away. The muffled choking sounds catch his attention, and he turns in time to see the last human choking as he vomits behind his gag.

Hugh takes a moment to bask in the terror in his eyes as he suffocates, as he slowly approaches the man.

Hugh unsheathes his claws and drags the razor sharp blades down the struggling man's thighs. The man bucks under his immense weight, eyes straining and bulging almost out of their sockets, as Hugh pushes his bulk down hard enough to hear bones break. Hugh spins, growling when he hears voices behind him.

"Jesus Christ, what are you? You couldn't just kill him?" asked the first human as Hugh begins to prowl towards his next prey.

"Hey, man, what the fuck? We are here together!" the second human exclaims once he notices he is being hunted.

The three men start backing away, and one of them pulls out a gun as his back hits the wall. Hugh crouches low as he prepares to strike. Bullets will not stop him.

"Hugh! Don't you even fucking think about it!" Sara's command reaches the human part of Hugh's brain as he turns towards his human ally. She is holding up her hand in an impatient manner as she speaks into her phone.

"You might want to get here soon. I've left you a present you will want to see," Sara purrs before disconnecting the call. She looks at him for a moment, her expression considering, before laughing high and bright. "Change back, Hugh. We need to get out of here."

DeMatteo ~ March 1, 11:41 p.m.

"DeMatteo, there seems to be a message here for you," Samantha calls out to him from the lower level.

DeMatteo turns away from the mangled corpses that are covered with the scent of his former lover Hugh. Any message seems redundant in the fact that Hugh could not have chosen a more brazen declaration than killing the leading members of the Human Council. If DeMatteo doesn't find him fast, the other Human Councils will surely declare war against the Santiago pride.

"Don't touch anything. Call the pride house. I want Sean in a safe room until I get home. Then call the Rivers pack; we are going to need the wolf enforcers here. And call our guy in the FBI. We need to keep the humans out of this," DeMatteo orders as he heads to the basement.

He hasn't been in this room since the trials, and he can admit that he is almost frightened of what he might find down there.

"DeMatteo, here on the back wall. It seems to be written in Councilman Reynold's blood," Samantha calls out from further by the cells.

DeMatteo prays that his instincts are wrong as a wave of foreboding washes across him, but his worst fears are confirmed when he stops is the same room in which he dispatched his parents' killers.

He can't fool himself into thinking all this is a coincidence when scrawled in Reynold's blood is a call for revenge.

THERE ARE RULES IN THE JUNGLE, EVEN FOR THE KING. BLOOD MUST BE REPAID IN BLOOD. I WILL HUNT YOU ALL DOWN, YOU ARE NOT SAFE ANYWHERE. I AM COMING FOR YOU!

The blood is still damp, and with his senses, DeMatteo can see the individual swirls and patterns of Sara's fingerprints in the detailed message left for him. She must have still been here in the building when she called Sean's cell phone, because DeMatteo had gathered a small hunting party and was on the premises in less than thirty minutes.

But her scent in this room is so potent DeMatteo knows that she waited. Sara had waited right here until there was a real possibility for them to pass one another before she fled. Everything about this has DeMatteo's lion bristling at such a bold and defiant challenge.

Chapter 9

March 1, 11:55 p.m.

"Sean, I need you to come to the safe room with me," Timothy had said when he ran into the den with his mate and Carla.

That had been nearly four hours ago, and it hadn't been until the door closed behind them that Timothy chose to inform him that only the Alpha would be able to open the door. And there hadn't been but one phone call from Samantha, almost an hour and a half ago, advising them that DeMatteo would be home shortly to get them out.

"How are you feeling?"

"Like I've been trapped inside this room for the last four hours!" Sean growls, his eyes flashing as he paces.

Every other step he alternates from being pissed DeMatteo had him locked into a safe room to terrified of what could have happened to cause this level of panic. Yes, Sean can accept that DeMatteo has taken protective to a level of crazy few could ignore, but never did Sean think that his mate would lock him in a bunker.

All of this is something Sean may have been able to write off as the Alpha just going a bit overboard, but the fact that DeMatteo has completely closed off their connection has his lioness whining and nervous.

"I am going to castrate your brother when he gets here," Sean says. He catches Kim trying to cover her mouth and winks.

These hormones are a bitch, and not being free to eat anything other than the dehydrated meat stored in the room is doing little to calm his cravings. The sound of footsteps catches his attention before the locks turn and the door opens, revealing an exhausted looking DeMatteo.

All thoughts of being pissed are forgotten as Sean runs to the Alpha, tucking in as close as the babies will allow.

"Where have you been? I've been so worried," Sean chokes out, horrified by the stinging in his eyes. DeMatteo just breathes him in deep, seemingly needing the comfort himself. Pulling back, DeMatteo wipes at the tears that have somehow escaped.

"I'm so sorry about locking you in here, baby," DeMatteo says, pulling him in close.

Sean watches DeMatteo pace around the office, trying to wait and let his mate find whatever words he is struggling with. After two or three failed starts, Sean finally snaps.

"So are you going to tell me what freaked you out so bad that you locked me in a closet, or am I going to have to beat it out of you? Trust me, now that I know you're safe, I'm leaning toward the latter so you might want to proceed with caution here." If Sean wasn't so scared of what DeMatteo was about to say, he would have laughed at the way DeMatteo is staring at him.

"Sara and Hugh are working together, and they attacked and killed several members of the Human Council, including the head elder," DeMatteo finally says. "They also left a message at the Council headquarters for me."

"Jesus. Was anyone left alive?" Sean asks. He has to take a seat as DeMatteo shakes his head. The babies react immediately; they seem especially sensitive to his emotions lately.

"There were at least three more humans, but I believe that Sara and Hugh now have others helping them. It would be impossible for just the two of them to get the drop on three highly-trained hunters. So I am guessing that whoever left that place alive is our enemy."

Sean's mouth waters, and his stomach rolls dangerously, as the cubs kick, twist, and flip frantically. He tries to soothe them through their bond, but they seem determined to kick his ribs in.

"Okay, what are we going to do? They left you a message? I can imagine what it said, so how are we going to finish the job?" Sean asks.

"I want to have a meeting with the Alpha Apex and Tien. I contacted your parents on my way home; they are going to move here. The pride is stronger when we're all together. Besides, if Sara realizes that she hasn't killed your mother, she might go back and try to finish the job."

"Thank you. I'll feel better with them here; god knows what that crazy bitch is going to try," Sean agrees easily. The waves of nausea have eased, the babies no longer feeling like they're going to claw their way out.

Sean's lioness still feels agitated; he can't help but to feel that he has forgotten something and left some kind of vulnerability that Hugh and Sara will eagerly exploit. It isn't until DeMatteo suggests they go for breakfast that Sean remembers a very easy target. "DeMatteo, what about Mary?"

"Sean, you know that we can't just tell humans about this."

"Who said anything about humans? I said I need to tell Mary, one human and my best friend. If Sara and Hugh are crazy enough to blow up your office and go up against the Human Council, what makes you think they won't go after my one weakness? My parents are moving here, so if they want to hurt me that only leaves Mary."

"They won't target humans; it is unheard of. The treaty…"

"Fuck the treaty, DeMatteo! I don't know if you've noticed it, but you are the only one worried about following the fucking rules!"

"Sean," DeMatteo starts but Sean has had enough. It is obvious that Hugh and the others don't give a fuck about the treaty, and playing by the rules is going to get them all killed. He doesn't know why, but Sean is sure that Mary will be their next target if he doesn't get her first.

"No, don't Sean me! I know that you are a fair Alpha, but these two are bug fuck crazy, and they don't seem to give a fuck who finds out about hunters, shifters, or any damn thing else. And so far, we have all been playing catch up because we are the only ones being hung up on the rules."

"DeMatteo, I have to say that I agree with Sean," Samantha announces as she walks into the room, surprising them both. Sean had been so consumed in convincing DeMatteo that he hadn't heard the other shifter's approach.

Samantha bares her neck to the Alpha Pair as her brother motions for her to continue. "Sara and Hugh have decided that they don't care about the rules, so we are going to have to play their game."

"I'm just worried. Once we expose her to the supernatural, we will have to take her under our protection. Uncle, you know that there will be humans and shifters in both Councils that will call for her to be brought into the pride or for her execution."

"What?" Sean stammers.

"Yes, there is a reason why we have been able to live amongst humans without any of them knowing. There are rules in the treaty about what humans can be told about us, and there are measures taken against those who stumble across it accidentally."

"So they kill humans that find out?"

"That has rarely happened. Most humans that find out are willing to either join the shifters or the Human Council. But your friend Mary is... She is a wildcard. There is no guarantee she will join us. I know she is your friend, but we have to be absolutely sure. It is not just us she can expose and put in danger."

"I know Mary can be hard to get, but other than you, she is one of the few people I would trust with my life."

"Okay then. It looks like our pride will be getting bigger," DeMatteo says, pulling Sean into an embrace.

Sunday, March 2, 8 a.m.

"Sean! Where the hell have you been? I haven't heard from you in a week. I was just about to drive out to that creepy ass house in the woods place you got going and kick your ass," Mary says by way of greeting.

"Hello, Mary, I miss you too. Funny you should say that; I was calling to see if you could come up for a visit? I can send a car to pick you up." Sean chuckles.

"Send me a car? Okay, Mr. Richie Rich, I can come up. It's eight in the morning. How about lunch?"

"Actually the car is already on the way. They should be there in about ten minutes," Sean hedges.

"Okay, that's a little creepy, but lucky for you I am already dressed. Tell me, is it one of those sexy ass bodyguards your husband had following you around?"

"Of course."

"Good man. I knew there was a reason we're best friends."

"Good. I'm glad our friendship can be of use to you. I'll see you in a few hours."

"Cheers." Sean takes a deep breath after ending the call.

That had gone better than he had hoped. He turns to face DeMatteo, who had been listening to the exchange.

"She is on her way. Now I just have to figure out how to tell my best friend that I have been lying to her for months. I mean, what am I supposed to say? 'Hey you remember my husband? Yeah, he can totally turn into a giant fucking lion. Oh and magic? totally real.'" Sean snorts dismissively at the thought.

There isn't any way to bring Mary into the pride without showing her how much a freak show his life has become. The more he thinks about how much he hasn't shared with her, the more Sean knows that this is going to end in tears.

"'Not only is magic real, but surprise, I'm supposedly the most magical person ever born, and before I forget, I'm pregnant! So what would you like for lunch?' Jesus Christ, DeMatteo, this is a fucking nightmare. Mary is going to freak or have a heart attack. No she's seriously going to freak the fuck out. Shit, I hope she doesn't bring her gun," Sean continues, the babies kicking out their displeasure at his rising blood pressure.

DeMatteo stays silent, just rubbing his shoulders, draining all the tension and stress that has been steadily building since he stepped outside that safe room. Sean leans into the touch, and the babies seem to also take comfort from the contact and calm inside him.

"Calm down, love, you're upsetting the babies. Besides this was your idea, and as you said, you are the most magical person ever born. I'm sure if you want to, you can hide your pregnancy. Hell, if you want to, you can make her stay and hide everything from her," DeMatteo suggests.

"No, I've kept this from her for too long. She is like family. If there is anyone I would ever trust enough to bring into the pride, it's Mary."

Sean rubs his belly nervously as he waits for Timothy to bring his oldest friend inside. It feels cowardly hiding behind the large desk but the chances of Mary passing out would be great if he just waddled out to meet her in all his pregnant glory.

DeMatteo doesn't know if humans were affected by Timothy's calming influence, but at this point Sean is eager to use anything to lessen the wrath of Mary.

Sure enough, Sean can hear his brother-in-law's easy tone as they approach. Sending up a quick prayer, Sean arranges himself in what he hopes is an inconspicuous manner. When the door opens, Mary just waltzes in in her usual manner, and suddenly Sean knows that everything will be okay.

Timothy catches his eye and Sean nods, letting the Omega know that he is ready to do this.

"Okay, I know I called you Richie Rich, but sending someone out to meet me was a bit much," Mary says as she takes a seat.

Timothy is already back outside the room, even though Sean knows the shifter will not stray far. The fact that DeMatteo has agreed to stay in his office is more than Sean can ask for.

"Well, I know how much you enjoy being pampered, so I figured I'd give you the full treatment." Sean laughs nervously, trying to fight down the panic he can feel building in his chest.

It's obvious that his attempts have failed when Mary's face shifts, hardening to her *don't fuck with me* expression.

"Since I am figuring that this is anything but a social call, how about we get right to it? I know you have been hiding something from me and since you've drug me here with no warning, I'm hoping it's because you've decided to start being honest," Mary accuses.

"You're right, and I'm sorry. But there isn't really an easy way to explain how much my life has changed…" Sean admits.

"Well, I've always been a jump right to it kind of girl so…" Mary leads. Sean knows he needs to just say it, but the longer he waits the less words come to mind.

"Okay." Sean takes a deep breath and just blurts everything together in one jumbled sentence. "Well, DeMatteo in a lion shifter, and I am a mage. We mated, and now I can also turn into a lion, and I'm pregnant with my first litter."

Looking up at his oldest friend, Sean's heart lunges painfully as Mary stares at him, blinking slowly. Her mouth opens after a second but closes just as suddenly as she searches his face.

After a few more unbearably tense seconds, she finally seems to remember how to speak, although her face is twisted in a well-deserved mask of confusion.

"You're telling the truth," she finally manages, looking for all the world like her entire world has burned around her.

Sean can hear her heart as it beats, her pulse racing at an almost alarming rate.

"Yes," Sean answers, even though it wasn't really a question.

Mary continues to stare, and the way her mouth opens and closes would be funny if Sean wasn't terrified that he could lose the person he loves like a sister. Then one of the babies chooses that moment to kick painfully at his bladder, making Sean grimace and rub his protruding belly to try to calm the party before the others decide to join in.

His movement must bring his distended belly into view because whatever trance Mary had been under breaks, and she is suddenly on her feet.

"Oh my god!" Mary rushes out as she practically falls over herself to get to Sean's side. "Holy shit, you're fucking pregnant!" Mary curses, her hand hovering just above his belly.

"Yeah, I am," Sean agrees softly, grabbing her hand and pressing it to his bump, the babies quickly kicking out their greeting against her palm. Timothy opens the door just as she is sinking to her knees. He smiles at the Omega as Mary steadily repeats 'oh god, oh god, oh god,' staring at her hand.

"Timothy, I think now would be a good time for those drinks. We have a lot of catching up to do," Sean says without taking his eyes off his friend.

Timothy enters silently, bringing with him a bottle of 1969 Domaine Leroy Clos de Vouget. Sean knows that Mary loved this vineyard, and while normally the insanely high cost would've put him off, Sean figures if there was ever a time to pull out the big guns this was it.

"Oh my god, Sean, this is unbelievable," Mary announces once they are alone again and the cubs have settled.

Sean can't help but laugh at that. With everything else that has happened with being kidnapped and finding out he's magic, being pregnant seems tame in comparison.

Mary shoots him an incredulous look at his laughter before smiling back down at his belly. Sean figures that since she hasn't passed out or run screaming from the room that now is as good a time as any to show her the real him.

"So, I'm guessing that this is why you are working from home now?" Mary asks, shakily getting to her feet.

Sean looks his closest friend in the eye before letting his magic slowly rise to the surface. He's careful to keep his claws retracted, but he knows his eyes are glowing brightly when he hears her suck in a breath.

Mary's eyes bulge so far for a moment that Sean is concerned they may fall out of her skull. Sean flashes what he hopes is a disarming smile, remembering too late about his fangs.

"What are you?" Mary whispers. He knows he's asking a lot, more than he should, but the fact that she has edged closer gives Sean hope.

"Well I'm still me. I'm still the same person you've known since childhood, but now I'm just more."

Chapter 10

Monday, March 11, 12 p.m.

"Uncle Richard, Aunt Tien, thanks for coming back on such short notice," DeMatteo says as he walks them to the main living room where everyone has gathered.

"So you know, I will be petitioning formally to bring a human into my pride. Her name is Mary. She is Sean's best friend, and we felt that she was in imminent danger."

"I can't imagine anyone will object, considering," Richard concedes as they enter the room.

Everyone is talking when they enter the room. DeMatteo finds Sean sitting in an arm chair next to Mary. It is obvious that all the stress is taking a toll on his mate; his skin is pale and his hands are twitching slightly as he strokes over their children. DeMatteo would give anything to take away everything that has happened to ruin what should be the happiest time in their lives.

"Uncle Richard, thank god you're here," Samantha exclaims, making her way over and throwing her arms around the older shifter.

"Samantha," Richard greets warmly.

"I hate to cut this short, but we really need to get this started. As we speak, we have no idea where Hugh and the hunter are hiding. The risk of them targeting the pride is too great to ignore. I am sure everyone here has had the chance to meet the newest member of our pride," DeMatteo says.

DeMatteo waits a beat before continuing. Retelling the events in graphic detail, it's imperative that he impresses on everyone the severity of the situation they are facing. Hugh and the hunter have ensured that every Council will be watching the outcome of this; should they fail; it is not just these two that might be gunning for the Santiago pride.

"Now that the Human Shifter Council is involved, I'm sure they will be calling for a quick capture. Too much of this is spilling out into the world, and we can't risk humans learning about our existence," DeMatteo explains.

Even Richard's position as Alpha Apex might be in danger, if other shifters deem them as too weak to hold their territory. Now with added humans to protect in the pride, DeMatteo is going to need his enforcers to double their efforts in securing the pride lands.

"Samantha, we need to secure the lands and provide security for the new unmated humans in our pride. We also need to set up video surveillance of the immediate surrounding areas."

"Yes, Alpha. I have already re-assigned Fredric and John as Mary's personal guards. They will protect her twenty-four hours a day. Rebecca and Frank have decided against having a shifter stand guard," Samantha begins.

"That is unacceptable. They need—" DeMatteo cuts in.

"Excuse me, Alpha, I mean no disrespect, but I am more than capable of protecting my husband. I am a pretty powerful spell caster. The only reason we agreed to move to the pride lands is we want to keep Sean calm. But I refuse to let that little girl and shifter run me underground. Besides, you are going to need every able bodied shifter patrolling the pride lands," Rebecca insists.

Everyone watches DeMatteo as he considers the witch's words, and after a silent conversation with the Alpha Mate, DeMatteo nods his acceptance. Samantha takes that as her cue to continue with the threat.

"With Sean's extra property, the pride lands have grown. We will need to set up additional cameras and security posts. I don't need to remind anyone how our lack of visual of that area has already been used by this hunter. I can't think of a reason why that area needs to be open. I want to restrict any shifter from visiting."

"That is going to be a problem," Sean cuts in. "My magic is tied to the land and I will need to visit the land daily until the birth. I will be traveling there tomorrow to complete the dedication to the Goddess. That land is a sacred space; it must be protected at all costs. I will also need some of the local flowers brought into the den before the birth."

Samantha looks to her Alpha, pleading wordlessly for him to intervene. DeMatteo simply nods to his mate, he will not second guess Sean's judgement, the message is clear: what the Alpha Mate says stands. Samantha looks like she is at a complete loss; DeMatteo knows there is no way they will be able to monitor this much land.

"Don't worry, Samantha. With the assistance of the Alpha Mate and his mother, I am sure we will be able to weave a magical protection over the lands. This will alert us of anyone who enters pride lands with evil intentions.

Normally I would set the wards to protect it, but with the Alpha Mate pregnant, it might use too much of his magic to sustain it," Tien adds.

DeMatteo can see the wheels turning in Sean's head. Sean sends him bits and pieces of his plan, and DeMatteo is floored at how sure his mate is in taking the lead.

"Well, I think we should head out immediately and start the wards. I can dedicate the temple to the Goddess, and that should give me a bit of a power boost," Sean says to the others.

"Just promise me you'll be careful. I want you to take guards with you in case you get distracted," DeMatteo says.

"We will take Samantha and Carla; I doubt anything will happen, but just in case. We will need a lunch and drinks for the Alpha Mate. We will take the Alpha Apex's vehicle. That thing has more protection than the president. Don't worry so much, Nephew. I will take care of your mate," Tien says as she heads to the door.

DeMatteo watches as the three magic users leave with their escorts in tow. It isn't until they are gone that

Richard speaks. "I will also send two of my private guards. They will need someone to drive."

The human's burst of laugher grabs DeMatteo, as he had almost forgotten she was in the room. Now that Sean is out of the house, DeMatteo figures this might be his only opportunity to speak with the woman privately. She has taken everything with a sense of ease that DeMatteo can't help but distrust.

DeMatteo searches their bond, and he is greeted with his mate's slight irritation at the additional security. He expected as much, but he assures his mate that they will stay out of his way. Once he is sure that his mate is in the vehicle and indeed headed to the pride lands, he focuses on the woman his mate seems so determined to protect.

"I apologize, Mary. I'm sure you can understand with everything going on, but normally there would be a warmer welcome to a new member of the pride," Richard addresses their new pride member.

DeMatteo tries to use his senses to gauge this woman. His lion seems almost fond of the person that his mate loves, but they have been tricked before. There is no way DeMatteo is going to allow another human to come in and try to destroy his family.

"Normally, there is a celebration and pride run to celebrate a new pride member, but I am sure you understand. With all the changes, we will have to delay the actual gathering," DeMatteo adds, noticing his uncle watching the human closely with a small smile stretched across his lips.

He feels a slight twinge of guilt for doing this without his mate's presence or approval, but as the Alpha of this pride, it is his duty to protect the members. Scenting the air, DeMatteo is first hit with the stench of his uncle's disapproval. The next scent, however, causes his hackles to rise, as Mary smells of nothing but rage.

"Understand?" Mary bellows, leaping from her seat.

DeMatteo's fangs erupt and his eyes flash red at the challenge; although he had scented her rising agitation, the hostile body language still startles him into action. Either insanity or an utter lack of self-preservation keeps the tiny human moving forward, not even flinching when his claws unsheathe. If anything, his display seems to egg the tiny human on.

"DeMatteo!" Richard stands, flashing his own eyes at his nephew. "Why don't we all take a few moments to calm down?"

DeMatteo takes a deep breath, trying to force his lion back under control. No doubt his mate will be less than pleased if DeMatteo attacks the woman he has fought hard to protect. The human in question must take his silence as a green light to continue because she barely takes a breath before continuing on her tirade.

As she continues to rant and rave, DeMatteo helplessly looks to his uncle, only to see the man's face turning an amazing shade of red. Clearly his uncle is enjoying his discomfort, trying and failing not to laugh as DeMatteo is taken to task by this tiny human female.

Mary ~

"No, I want to get back to what it is that I am supposed to understand. Please explain to me exactly what it is that you think I should understand. Is it the fact that you are some kind of freaky shapeshifter? Or maybe it's how and why you've forced my best friend to lie to me? Oh I know, you want me to understand why you have put Sean's life in danger? Because *no*, I don't fucking understand! Why don't you explain it to me?" Mary fumes.

She doesn't even realize she is moving until she is poking the giant man in front of her. On any other day Mary might be afraid, but right now all she can see is the man that has stolen her best friend and may be the cause of his death.

No, right now all Mary can do is not grab her gun and put a few bullets in his ass. Not that she wants to kill him, but she does want to punish him.

"Oh you've got yourself a hell of a human with that one, Nephew." The older man laughs.

Mary grits her teeth so tightly she is surprised she hasn't crushed a molar as she glares at him.

"Listen, I don't know who the hell you are, and I don't really care. All I want to know is what the hell you got Sean involved in. He was just a normal human before DeMatteo showed up, and while I don't know why his parents seem to be fooled by your bullshit, I will make it my life's mission to protect him."

"I am Richard, and while I appreciate your strength, let me assure you that Sean was always so much more than human. I understand that you are scared, but make no mistake that DeMatteo will protect his mate from any and every one."

"Are you threatening me..." Mary begins, but Richard powers on.

"Absolutely not. I am merely advising you of the circumstances you now find yourself in, and I would hate for you and my nephew to have any misunderstandings. Sean loves you; therefore, everyone in this pride will do whatever it takes to protect you, but I ask that you try."

For all intents and purposes, Mary is left speechless. Richard is actually a carbon copy of DeMatteo, only older and more refined, but there is something in his eyes that makes her want to trust the shifter.

While she still might not understand everything that has happened, Mary has always trusted her gut, and her gut trusts Richard. But that didn't mean she doesn't have questions.

Since her arrival, both Sean and his husband, (*mate?*), had avoided telling her exactly what was going on. Why they were all in danger, and she admits that she has not been on her best game. First the shock of finding out that not only had her best friend married a guy that turned into a lion, but he is also magic, and that wasn't even the biggest mind fuck they had for her.

Oh no, Sean also showed her that somehow he was pregnant, with triplets! So it hadn't been hard for them to avoid explaining what else was going on, but now that she has more or less come to grips with the concept of magic, a pregnant man, and shapeshifters, she wants answers.

"Yes, and it will be better for everyone involved if you explain to me exactly what type of danger is coming after Sean and what we are doing to protect him," Mary states.

Holding her ground and boldly looking her new Alpha in the eyes, she refuses to back down. DeMatteo huffs out a breath before giving a quick nod and taking a seat. As soon as he starts talking Mary realizes that she has been woefully unprepared for the gravity of what was facing them.

Chapter 11

April 1, 7 a.m.

"There should be a law banning the torture of pregnant people," Sean complains, trying to get into one of the nearly impossible yoga poses Mary has insisted is good for the babies.

He is almost convinced that this is some form of payback Mary deviously has disguised as "exercise." The last few weeks have been anything but easy as his mate and best friend skirt around one another like a couple of back alley cats looking for a fight.

Trying to get them to engage in less that hostile conversations has been an exercise in patience that Sean just doesn't have.

"Stop bitching. You need to keep your muscles loose. Yoga is excellent for pregnant women," Mary jokes, laughing at his scandalized face and "I'm not a girl" reply. This has become their routine, and he'd be lying if he said he wasn't grateful that she is helping him through this.

"So today is the big day. Think you'll finally find out what you're having?" Mary asks, handing him his water bottle; the sign that his torture session is done for the day.

"I hope so," Sean agrees, taking the offered water and downing it all in one go. "Tien told me during my mating ceremony that she saw all boys in a vision, but I want the confirmation."

"I can't even imagine, but then again, I keep waiting to wake up from this craziness," Mary says. Sean can feel his stomach drop, and suddenly he needs to get away before he bursts into tears.

Even though Mary has pretty much taken everything in stride and has tried to make a home in the pride, Sean still fears that one day she might resent him for dragging her into constant danger.

Something must show on his face because suddenly Mary grabs his arm before he can escape to another room.

"Hey, what's wrong?" Mary asks urgently.

Sean can feel his eyes burning, tears threatening to escape. He could easily overpower the woman to get away, but even his lioness is mewling in distress at the thought of losing Mary.

"I'm sorry I dragged you into this. I know I'm asking you to accept a lot and to change your whole life by joining the pride, and I know that it's not fair, but I need you. You are my best friend, my sister, and I need you here. I know you hate DeMatteo and being told what to do, but he just wants to keep you safe, and the safest place for you to be right now is on pride lands. I know it's selfish because by trying to protect you I've pulled you into more danger," Sean admits, and fighting the tears is useless.

Mary pulls him into her arms and shushes him; tears and sweat meet where his face is tucked into her shoulder, but he can't seem to make himself care.

"Sean, first of all, you didn't drag me anywhere. I was given a choice, and I chose to stay and join the pride. I want to be here. You're my family, and I will do anything to keep you safe. Secondly, there is no such thing as you being selfish. You are the kindest, most giving person I've ever met. And last, I don't hate DeMatteo. I could never hate anyone that has made you so happy," Mary insists, holding him close.

Sean's lioness purrs inside his head, sensing nothing but honesty from the human. After pulling himself together, Sean looks up at his sister. Her smile is nothing but loving and suddenly Sean is mortified at what she must be thinking about his latest breakdown.

"Sorry for all the hysterics. I swear this pregnancy has turned me into a neurotic headcase," Sean mutters, using his towel to clean his face.

"I don't mind you being a hormonal mess," Mary jokes as Sean rolls his eyes. He is forever grateful for whatever deity that saw fit to send Mary into his life. She is his anchor to the normal world; if there is one person Sean can rely on to keep him grounded, it is this petite hellcat.

"I'll remember that when you're pregnant," Sean retorts, snorting at the look of pure horror on Mary's face.

"Pregnant? Me? Yeah, no thank you," Mary denies, grabbing her own towel, but Sean can sense her panic is tinged with sadness.

"Don't you want to have children?" he asks, deciding to press. They have been friends for decades, but for the first time Sean realizes that they've never discussed the subject of family where it pertains to Mary.

"Kids? Who knows? First I'd need a boyfriend, and in case you haven't noticed, I don't have anyone beating down my door for the position," Mary dismisses. Sean is about to disagree when she cuts him off. "But enough about me. You need to shower and get ready for your check-up and I have a dozen briefs to catch up with." Though her tone is joking, Sean can tell he has unknowingly touched on a sensitive topic.

So instead of pushing, Sean nods in easy acceptance; he doesn't need to sense her emotions to know that for the moment this subject is closed, but it is something he will bring up again.

"Yeah, I definitely need a shower and something to eat," he says before heading back into the pride house.

Mary just waves him off, and Sean can't help but wonder why the thought of children upsets her so much. Maybe it is something he can speak with his mother about, but later. He wasn't joking when he said he needed to eat.

DeMatteo is waiting for him in their bathroom, and judging by the worry lines creasing his face, it is obvious that he has heard at least part of their conversation outside. To say the stress of adding Mary to the pride has affected the Alpha would be an understatement. Sean has tried unsuccessfully to convince his mate that Mary isn't a threat to the pride, but DeMatteo has doggedly kept her at arm's length, and their constant bickering is starting to take its toll.

"I'm gonna shower then grab something to eat before Timothy arrives," Sean says in lieu of a greeting.

There is no way he is getting into another battle of wills with the shifter; after Mary he just doesn't have the will to fight.

"I'll bring you a plate," DeMatteo offers, watching him carefully as he pulls off his clothes. The usual curl of desire sparks to life in his belly and he slows his movements down, making a show of pulling off his clothes before walking over to his mate.

Once he is close, Sean doesn't hesitate to push into the Alpha's space, wrapping his arms around the larger man. DeMatteo isn't the only one who takes comfort in their combined scent and the need to reconnect. But other than blow jobs and a few rushed handies, DeMatteo hasn't seemed eager to take their flagging sex life to the next level.

Refusing to sour the mood with questions, Sean accepts the physical comfort for what it is. "Thanks, and I am okay," Sean says, brushing a kiss to DeMatteo's neck.

"Okay, and I'm sorry. I'll work on being around Mary. I don't hate her, and I don't want you to be stressed."

"That's good. You two just need to give each other a break," Sean says fondly, stepping away. DeMatteo responds with the tiniest of nods before heading towards the door.

April 1, 1:30 p.m.

"So how have you been feeling?" Timothy asks, spreading the ultrasound gel on his belly.

With all the advanced medical equipment laying around, one wouldn't think it would have been a financial stretch to purchase a warmer for the translucent gel. Nothing fancy, just enough to make it not frigid before putting it directly on a pregnant person.

"God, Timothy! Where do you keep that shit, the freezer?" Sean grits out while Timothy pushes the wand harder, searching for what, he had no clue.

"Is it too cold? Funny, none of the women have ever complained before."

"Oh really?" Sean snorts.

"Nope, but I have something that will make it worth it. Take a look at those babies," Timothy replies, turning the monitor.

On the screen there is a tangle of paws and tails. It is impossible to tell where one baby ends and the others begin. Sean senses his mate approaching the room long before the door opens.

Taking his place beside Sean, DeMatteo sucks in a breath as he gets a first real look at their cubs. And Sean is convinced that he is witnessing the most amazing thing to ever exist on this planet.

"God, baby, look at them," DeMatteo gushes. Normally Sean would tease him about not being the big bad Alpha, but at this moment Sean agrees with the sentiment.

"Yeah. I am so glad you made it," Sean reaches up to grab DeMatteo's hand when Timothy twists a few knobs and a chorus of sprinting heartbeats fills the room.

There had been an emergency phone call while he was in the shower; the wife of one of DeMatteo's clients had tried to take their children out of the country without her husband's consent. Luckily DeMatteo was able to get a judge to issue an order restricting the minor's passport over the phone and giving the husband temporary custody until the next hearing.

"I wouldn't have missed this for the world," DeMatteo whispers as he squeezes Sean's hand. And Timothy was so right; this right here, made everything he has been through worth it.

"I can print out a few pictures. You know the pride will be dying to see the Alpha Pair's first litter. Three strong Beta identical triplets, and I can inform you that they are all indeed males. Amazing," Timothy says, clicking buttons.

Sean is so consumed with watching the three tiny lions move that he almost misses the sound of awe. Almost.

"Is that strange, that they are identical? I thought three was the most common birth number?" Sean asks.

"Strange? No, I've read about it in the archives," Timothy says, but there is just enough something there to make Sean push. Not what he said, but more of what he isn't saying.

"Yeah, have you delivered identical triplets?"

"No. Um, no one has. There is only one story of identical triplets being born and they died during the great wars," Timothy answers.

"Were they soldiers?" Sean asks, and with the way Timothy's shoulders hunch over, he knows the answer before Timothy begins to speak.

"No, the humans burned them and their mother alive shortly after the births."

Sean and DeMatteo share a look, and they don't need their mating bond to know what the other is thinking. It doesn't take a genius to see the parallel; they may not be at war but they have their own crazy human bent on hunting them.

"But enough about the tragic past. Let's see if you've started shifting internally," Timothy says, and being reminded that their children may be born any day is enough to break the overcast that has overshadowed the last few minutes.

Sean strips while Timothy rolls the machines and other equipment out of the room. Sean's lioness is completely at ease with the proceedings now that they have switched his exams to the den.

"So have you been feeling any pains? Cramping?" Timothy asks, all while he has not one but two fingers shoved deeply into Sean's opening.

"Um, a little, I think. Although I wouldn't really call it pain, just uncomfortable," Sean stutters out.

After everything he's seen and done since meeting DeMatteo and the other shifters, this should not make him blush, but Sean can feel the blood in his face as he tries to focus on answering Timothy's questions.

"I see. Let me know if anything changes. The birth canal is now fully formed. So that means you could go into labor at any time."

"God, I hope so. I can't wait to get these hellraisers out," Sean jokes, giving DeMatteo's hand a squeeze.

Even though every day has been leading up to this, Sean is nervous about the birth. Not just the fact that he had grown a magic vagina, *okay, that still kind of freaks him out*, but the thought of having three sons.

"Well, everything looks good. I would stay close to the den and call me the minute you feel like you have to shift," Timothy says, taking off his gloves.

Sean scurries to the shower when DeMatteo walks over to the door. He's heard everything he needs to know; now he just needs to get the feeling of the other shifter's touch off his body.

The fact that it's Timothy, their Omega, does nothing to ease his lioness's insistence. He takes his time, making sure to scrub away every trace of Timothy's scent. It's just one more strange habit Sean chalks up to his lioness getting pissier and pissier as he gets closer to the due date.

DeMatteo is waiting when he steps out of the shower, towel in hand, and at this point Sean doesn't even bother to put up a token protest. Sean leans against his Alpha, letting the other man hold up his weight, as he gently dries his skin. This has become their routine, DeMatteo whispering to his belly as he smoothes lotion on Sean's skin.

DeMatteo's need to take care of him and the cubs has grown to the point of redefining obsessive. Sean was honestly surprised his overbearing Alpha had let him shower alone; he must have been drowning Timothy in endless questions to have left him alone so long.

If it wasn't for the fact that Sean can feel every bit of love and caring his mate puts into every action, he might be upset that the man didn't trust him to not somehow kill himself in their den. DeMatteo drops to his knees to lotion his legs and Sean's dick immediately takes notice of his proximity.

"I want you to fuck me," Sean blurts out.

It's not like they aren't intimate, but he can sense his mate's reluctance to fuck him. As much as he knows it's just DeMatteo's need to protect the cubs, Sean would be lying if he tried to say it didn't hurt.

DeMatteo freezes, mouth inches away from Sean's steadily growing erection, before backing away and looking up at him. Sean knows what he is about to say before the words leave his unfairly perfect mouth. "I don't think that's a good idea."

Sean's eyes burn as he is rejected by his Alpha. He refuses to cry, instead reaching for his indignation.

"You don't think... Why the hell not, DeMatteo? Are you not attracted to me like this?" Sean knows it's the hormones making him feel like this, but as his weight balloons, he can't help but to feel insecure.

While Sean has never been as fit or muscular as DeMatteo, in the last month he had developed what could only be called breasts, and he can't even remember the last time he had been able to see his feet.

"I just need you to tell me. Do you still want me?" Sean asks, choking back a sob.

Even his lioness is letting out heartbreaking yowls at the thought of losing their mate. Hurt and anger bubble together as he flinches away, waddling as fast as his legs will take him, fleeing to the safety of their den without even bothering to get dressed.

Sean isn't surprised when DeMatteo lets him leave the room; his mate's shock and sadness is leaking through their bond, but his own shame and resentment burn hot enough to make him not care.

By the time he has finally made it to their nest, DeMatteo is reaching out, gripping his elbow to help him lower his bulk onto the mattress. Hot tears finally break free as Sean watches his mate kneel at his feet.

DeMatteo ~

DeMatteo is instantly on his feet, following his obviously upset mate. His lion roars in his head that he needs to fix this. He can feel the waves of misery and rejection flowing through their bond, leaving him reeling in the knowledge that he has caused his mate to feel this way.

Sean goes directly to the safety of his nest, and DeMatteo doesn't hesitate to help him sit on the bed. Reaching out to grasp his arm, DeMatteo is grateful when his mate doesn't recoil from the touch. Once he is seated, DeMatteo falls to his knees, desperate for his mate to understand.

He babbles in his rush to explain, "Of course I am! How could you even think...? Sean, you are carrying my cubs. There is no way for you to be more desirable than you are right now. It's just that you are so close to the delivery, and so much has happened, I just can't... The thought of hurting you or the cubs."

"You won't hurt us. I need you."

"I'm sorry. I never want you to question this."

"I know I'm being ridiculous. But you never seem to want to touch me, this last month... I just, I look at my body…" Sean breaks off miserably. DeMatteo doesn't need their bond to feel his mate's despair.

DeMatteo pushes his nose in the juncture between Sean's dick and thigh, taking in the thick scent of his mate's arousal, only made more potent by the scent of his proven fertility.

"Fuck, Sean, how do you not know what seeing you round with my cubs does to me?" DeMatteo asks. Pride fills him as Sean's cock begins to stir; there is never a time DeMatteo can imagine his body not responding to the other man.

"I want you to fuck me," DeMatteo says before licking up his mate's cock, watching it harden under his ministrations.

"You want me to fuck you?" Sean gasps out, his legs spreading instinctively and giving DeMatteo better access.

DeMatteo can't help but chuckle. "Yeah. I know you can smell how hard I am; how much I want to sit on your dick."

"Fuck, DeMatteo! You can't just say shit like that to me." Sean pants, but DeMatteo isn't planning on talking.

The thought that his mate wondered if the Alpha still wanted him has DeMatteo's lion itching to get out to claim their mate.

"Shit, I can't even see my dick, not to mention touch it," Sean groans as DeMatteo slides his fingers in Sean's crack. His mate's heart stutters as his fingers trace his hole before falling back into the bed.

Taking that as his cue to continue, DeMatteo dips his fingers inside to gather some of the slick dripping from his mate, soaking his hand to the wrist before reaching behind himself to stretch his ass. He is rewarded by Sean's strangled moan as he props himself on his elbows to watch.

It's been so long since he's done this that his grip tightens on Sean's cock at the burn as he shoves two fingers into himself. Sean doesn't just watch for long; by the time DeMatteo has added a third finger, his mate is scooting up the bed, his eyes flashing.

Prepped enough, DeMatteo gets to his feet. Sean's dick is flushed, straining against his belly, and DeMatteo is floored by how sexy the other man looks carrying his cubs.

"Well, I can definitely see it. Why don't you just lie back and let me ride you? Let me show you how much I want you," DeMatteo husks as he crawls onto the bed and slips his fingers back inside of his mate. Gathering some more slick, DeMatteo strokes Sean's cock once from root to tip and takes a second to figure out how to make this work.

Unsurprisingly, it is Sean who comes up with the solution. "Shit, DeMatteo. Turn around and fuck yourself on my cock, reverse cowboy," Sean groans, spreading his legs a little.

Once he gets turned around, DeMatteo doesn't waste any time before grabbing his mate's cock and aiming at his hole. It's a tight fit, but once the blunt tip pops through those tight muscles, it's a smooth slide until DeMatteo is settled in Sean's lap.

Both men moan at the sensation of Sean's cock buried to the hilt. Resting his hands on Sean's knees, DeMatteo slowly pulls himself up before shoving back faster. Sean's eager shout forces DeMatteo to clench hard before repeating the motion.

DeMatteo has to focus on the slight amount of pleasure he can already feel rolling through him. The burn of penetration and too little prepping makes each roll of his hips feel like he might tear apart.

"You okay?" Sean asks, obviously feeling his conflicting emotions through their bond. DeMatteo can only nod as fire races up his spine at his quickened descent.

After a few more bounces, DeMatteo's tongue finally unsticks as he groans out, "Yeah… Just forgot how big your cock is."

In response Sean grabs his hips, and DeMatteo can feel the tell prick of claws as Sean grinds up into his body. DeMatteo groans, gripping his mate's legs to quicken his pace.

"Jesus! Yes, DeMatteo. That's it, fuck me, baby," Sean encourages. After that, there aren't many words. Just hard panting and the slap, slap, slap of flesh as sweat begins to roll down the Alpha's back.

DeMatteo gasps when he arches his back just right, forcing his mate's cock where he really needs it. Sean chooses that moment to shove his hips up, and DeMatteo is almost sobbing.

It doesn't take long for them to pick up a rhythm. Sean thrusting his hips up every time DeMatteo descends, and honestly DeMatteo is surprised how much force Sean is using with his belly in the way.

"Damn it, Sean, not gonna last long," DeMatteo moans out after a particularly devastating thrust. He has to fight to keep his claws from coming out, his grip tightening on Sean's knees with each slide.

Sean is hitting his prostate with every thrust, and he is balancing on the edge of too much, not enough. At this rate he won't even need to touch his cock. He can already feel the orgasm gathering like a storm in his belly.

"Me too. Yeah, just like that. Grind on that cock," Sean all but growls when DeMatteo slams down. Clenching and grinding, Sean's cock rubs mercilessly on that sensitive bundle of nerves.

"God… DeMatteo, I'm gonna!" Sean wails and DeMatteo clenches down brutally as he too is swept away.

Each pulse of his mate's release seems to beat on his prostate, prolonging his orgasm. Minutes, hours, or years could have passed as DeMatteo's vision whited out.

Sean ~

"God, DeMatteo! That was amazing," Sean wheezes out as the spasms of his orgasm tighten and clench his belly.

DeMatteo shifts slightly before pulling away, the slick pop and the rush of cum Sean can feel running down his balls does little to break him out of the orgasmic haze he is floating on.

"Let me clean you up," DeMatteo offers, but Sean's not ready to part just yet.

"Stay," he says, and amazingly the Alpha doesn't argue, instead just crawling up to lie beside him.

"Yeah, I've missed this. I'm sorry I hurt you, hurt us, it's just…" DeMatteo starts, but Sean isn't interested in placing blame. He is just happy to reconnect with his Alpha.

"Enough. We discussed this, you apologized, and I accepted it. So stop fucking up my afterglow," Sean teases before nuzzling and licking at the nipple in front of him.

"I don't know what I ever did to deserve you."

"Me neither. But feel free to thank me like this anytime you want."

"I love you," DeMatteo whispers reverently, and Sean can't help but smile at the other man. DeMatteo might not be the type to bring him flowers or write poetry, but even without the bond, his emotions are easy to feel almost like a physical touch.

"I love you too, but now I need another shower and I am going to need to be fed."

"Yes, dear," DeMatteo quips.

"Hey now, don't be like that. It's your brood that needs the nutrition." Sean glares, but the fondness even he can hear in his voice no doubt tells the Alpha how he really feels.

Chapter 12

May 8th, 2 a.m. Month Ten ~ Finish line

"I like trying to get pregnant, I'm not so sure about childbirth." ~ Lauren Holly

"DeMatteo!" Sean shouts as he doubles over in pain.

The frantic cries of the triplets are making it impossible to communicate with DeMatteo through their bond. It feels as if they are trying to claw their way through his flesh. He needs to shift; his lioness is scratching at his brain telling him it is time.

"Oh my god! DeMatteo, get in here!" Sean moans as he attempts to strip. His skin feels too tight, and itchy as his fur begins to cover his skin.

The only thing keeping him human is his need for his mate to be here to protect him and their young. He will be too vulnerable during the birth. Dragging himself to the nest they have set up on the floor, Sean finally shreds the last of his clothing with his extended claws as DeMatteo bursts into their den.

"Sean! Sean, what happened? Are you okay?" DeMatteo asks as he looks wildly around the room.

"Oh god…" Sean starts but his words are cut short by another wave of pain. "No, I'm not okay! I think the cubs are just ready to come out..." He continues once he is able to form words.

"Come out? Are you sure?"

"Shit! Yes, I'm sure! Get Timothy! Now! I need to shift!" Sean literally roars before curling around his distended belly. Sean's body twists, bones crack, and muscles reshape, as his heavily pregnant lioness comes forward.

DeMatteo is torn between going to call his brother and staying with his mate; his lion is growling at the thought of leaving their mate. Timothy must have sensed his panic through the pride bond, because he appears at the den's door, bag in hand, releasing DeMatteo from having to make the choice.

"The cubs are coming," DeMatteo gets out around a mouthful of fangs as Timothy enters the den.

Sean has completely shifted into his lioness by the time DeMatteo starts to pull off his own clothes. DeMatteo isn't sure if he is ready, but his lion is more than eager as he rips his way to the surface.

Timothy ~

Timothy drops his bags and immediately goes over to Sean. His lion has been anxious all day, so he wasn't that surprised when he felt Sean's distress through the pride bond. Sean is already shifted and pacing in his nest, and Timothy can tell by his gait that the contractions have escalated greatly since his last exam.

"Hello, Sean. I see you're ready to deliver. I'm going to need to move your tail to examine the birth canal, okay?" Timothy asks, even though he knows the Alpha Mate can't answer in this form.

Timothy cuts his eyes to his Alpha. DeMatteo is pacing nervously on Sean's other side. Although Timothy has delivered at least five cubs, everything is more intense when there is a fully shifted Alpha Male watching your every move, even if that Alpha is your brother.

Timothy is under no misconception that this is a delicate situation. Had Sean been a full shifter, Timothy wouldn't be allowed near this birth. Alphas are notoriously violent to anyone perceived to be a threat to their mate or cubs.

"Alpha, I am going to need to examine Sean. I'm guessing it won't be long before we have our first cub," Timothy tells DeMatteo, hoping to remind him that he is here to help get the cubs delivered safely.

Not surprisingly, DeMatteo just huffs in annoyance at his commentary. Timothy focuses on sending out calming pheromones before attempting to touch the Alpha Mate. Timothy runs his hands down Sean's side, feeling for the contractions.

"Okay, here we go," Timothy announces as he grabs the base of Sean's tail.

The birth canal is clearly visible now, indicating that Sean has begun to dilate. As Timothy inserts two fingers feeling for the cub's position, a strong contraction grips his fingers, and he can feel the crown of the first cub's head. He carefully pulls his fingers from Sean. The first cub is ready to be born and he will need his tools.

DeMatteo ~

DeMatteo fights not to growl as Timothy checks his
mate's readiness, and as soon as he steps away DeMatteo
takes his place. DeMatteo scents the air, taking in the subtle
changes in his mate's scent. The woodsy scent he had
detected earlier has magnified significantly and the animal
part of his brain is drawn to it.

Sean yowls in pain, and DeMatteo can see where
his muscles tighten, causing his birth canal to open slightly.
It allows a thin, bloody, mucus filled discharge to seep out,
and DeMatteo instinctively laps it away. Needing to keep
his mate clean in preparation for the birth, he senses
Timothy's return as more and more of the fluid starts to
flow out.

"That is normal; it will continue throughout the
birth. I am going to need to get in here. If you can stand by
Sean's head while he pushes, your presence should be
enough to help him push the babies out," Timothy
encourages, though DeMatteo suspects he is simply trying
to convince him that he will be of more use than he actually
is.

DeMatteo circles Sean and sets about grooming his
face. It doesn't take much to see that Sean's body is already

working hard trying to birth their cubs. DeMatteo chuffs out constant encouragements as Sean starts to yowl low in his throat.

"Okay. Sean, I can see the head, keep pushing," Timothy says as Sean leans heavily on DeMatteo.

Lions give birth standing, but Sean is using DeMatteo as a lean-to as he pushes. Because of their height, Timothy will need to catch the cubs before they fall to the ground, mostly in case they are born in their more fragile human form.

DeMatteo braces himself against Sean's constant pushing as his pain filled yowls turn into a near constant growl. Timothy is chanting out directions to push, and DeMatteo wishes he could be down there to see when his son makes his way into the world.

"Okay, here comes cub number one. Push, push, push, push. Great job, Sean!" Timothy shouts joyfully as he lays the first cub gently on the ground.

Sean immediately lies on his side to reach the cub, where he carefully chews through the umbilical cord and begins to clean what is left of the bag of water that once surrounded the cub. DeMatteo finally gets to walk down and greet his cub as Sean pants through the contractions of delivering the cub.

"The cub feels like about eleven pounds," Timothy says as he backs away from them.

DeMatteo is mesmerized by the tiny squirming bundle of joy. He is absolutely perfect; his coat is light brown and speckled. Sean adjusts to allow him to nurse when the cub starts making these pathetic whimpering sounds, and DeMatteo just melts.

This tiny, blind, defenseless cub is the most beautiful thing DeMatteo has ever seen, and he just knows that his life will always be devoted to protecting his mate and cubs.

"Looks like you are getting more uncomfortable," Timothy says about a half an hour later when Sean starts fidgeting restlessly.

DeMatteo had noticed both Sean and the cub starting to make tiny distressed sounds for the last few moments. It seems as if cub number two is now ready to join his family on the outside.

"Sean, maybe DeMatteo should take cub one over to the nest while you push," Timothy suggests as he puts down fresh towels.

DeMatteo is over instantly, using his snout to gently prod his son further away from Sean so he can pick him up. Sean growls in warning as the cub yips at DeMatteo's manhandling. Undeterred, DeMatteo grips his cub's fur in his teeth.

It takes some maneuvering, but he gets the uncooperative ball of fur to the nest and lays him on the fur blankets.

"There we go, Sean; it looks like you are ready to push out cub number two," Timothy says, pulling DeMatteo's attention away from his son.

It's difficult, but he leaves him nestled in the blankets. His human mind knows that both Sean and the cub are safe here inside the pride house.

Almost every member of the pride in or around the pride land is providing around the clock security. But the events of the past few months are all front and center in DeMatteo's mind, leaving his lion near feral in its need to protect their family.

Chapter 13

"Last one, Sean. You are doing so well!" Timothy praises as he moves Sean's tail to get a better view of his opening.

Sean pants as pain radiates up his spine as his uterus contracts. He can't stop the yowls of pain that escape with each push. This time, it feels like only seconds pass before he feels the now familiar burn of his flesh stretching to its limits around the large cub.

"That's it, Sean! Big push, big push, almost there!" Timothy coaches as he prepares to help birth the final cub.

Timothy helps as best he can, pushing and pulling on the tissues around the furry head as baby number three enters the world. This one is also fully shifted, and feels to weigh about eight pounds. He's much smaller than the two older cubs, but large by human standards.

Once the last cub is delivered, Sean chews through the umbilical cord and begins to clean the fluids from his son's fur. Sean pants as more contractions tighten his frame, and the cubs all start whimpering as Sean yowls out in pain as the placenta is pushed from his body.

It is almost as large as their biggest cub. Being identical, all three babies had been attached to this organ. When it is finally free from his body, Sean sniffs it, testing to make sure the babies were healthy. Once his inspection is complete, Sean begins to eat the afterbirth just like his wild cousins, not wanting to leave a trace of the new birth.

Exhausted, Sean grabs his youngest by the scruff and heads over to where DeMatteo is still guarding their other cubs. It takes a few seconds of nudging the cubs before he finally lies down in the nest to nurse his cubs.

DeMatteo gently sniffs at each cub, scenting them, as they root around Sean's belly searching for a nipple. It's impossible in this form to help them other than nudging at them with his nose. After what seems like an eternity, Sean has them each on a tit.

The feeling of having his sons nurse from his breast is a little more than strange, causing his belly to tighten painfully with each pull. Listening to the wet sucking sounds, Sean's lioness purrs in happiness. They've done it. Each of the cubs are here and safe and there isn't one thing Sean would ever change. This is perfect.

Timothy ~

From a distance, Timothy watches as the Alpha Pair settles in with the cubs. The entire birth had only taken a few hours, even though first time mothers normally take at least a day to birth a litter. But just like with everything else, Sean is the exception to the rule.

Timothy wonders if it was his magic that made the birth uncomplicated, and he makes a note to question Tien about this.

Timothy can feel his lion slipping closer to the surface; as an Omega, his lion is a natural caregiver and is wired to care for the pride. Gathering his supplies, Timothy continues to exude his calming and healing pheromones.

Once his gear is stored in his bags and placed by the door, Timothy focuses on cleaning his Alpha's den as best he can.

In the wild, a lioness would give birth alone in a hidden den, far from any other predators. She would clean any trace of the birth, attempting to hide the scent of blood and birth that would be a sign to others that there was easy prey available.

For the first few weeks after the birth, both the lioness and her cubs are at their most vulnerable, and even though they are shifters and these threats are uncommon, they cannot fight their instincts.

Timothy gathers the soiled and bloodied linens from the floor. He knows the Alpha Pair will not allow him to remain in the den for much longer. Normally he would insist on weighing and checking the cubs immediately, but that would be a fatal mistake with an Alpha Pair.

He would have to wait until DeMatteo and Sean called on him before attempting to touch the Alpha's cubs.

He is satisfied for now with the sounds of the cubs eagerly nursing; any further examination would be too dangerous to attempt. This being the first litter, DeMatteo's lion will be extremely protective to the point of being irrational.

Timothy is careful to only take side glances, making sure to stay as small as possible.

Once they are finished, Timothy watches as Sean begins to carefully, meticulously clean each cub. Any doubts he may have had about the former human's ability to care for the cubs is cured as he watches the tender exchange between mother and cub.

Timothy is surprised it takes until he begins mopping the floor before his Alpha demands his departure. DeMatteo is beginning to eye him suspiciously as he chuffs at his cubs, and Timothy can feel DeMatteo's irritation at his presence. Wanting to avoid causing an attack, Timothy decides to leave the last of the mess for the Alpha Pair to clean on their own.

"The Alpha Mate and the cubs are doing great. They are resting in the den with three boys and no complications," Timothy announces to the entire pride that has gathered in and around the pride house.

"When do you think we will be allowed to see them?" someone asks. Timothy shakes his head; this question is expected, but everyone knows that Alpha Pairs tend to take longer to introduce their cubs to the pride.

"I don't know." It's the only answer he can give them, and even though it is not what anyone wants to hear, it is the truth. Samantha finally steps forward, Goddess bless her, to address the pride.

"While we are all excited about the birth of the cubs, we need to keep our vigil up in protecting the pride lands. We can all feel the new members to the pride, and I am sure the Alpha will hold a ceremony to bring the cubs to the pride. Now I need each of you to go back to your post. There are still unknown enemies out there, and now we have even more reason to ensure no threats enter," Samantha commands.

As the head enforcer, it falls to her to lead the pride while the Alpha is away. Timothy silently thanks every deity known to man that this task will never fall to him. As the pride starts to disperse, Timothy heads to his office to document the births and contact the Alpha Apex. Richard answers on the first ring; no doubt that he too felt the new pride members.

"How are they?" Richard asks.

"Everyone is doing well. The births went quickly and there were no complications. They are all resting in the den. Is Aunt Tien there? I have a few questions for her," Timothy reports.

"Sure, I'll put you on speaker," Richard says, and Timothy listens as he calls for his mate.

"Hello, Timothy. You have questions?" Tien asks, joining in the conversation.

"Just a few. I was wondering if Sean's magic could explain how he birthed all three in less than five hours. As I am sure you know, most first time mothers can take almost a day to birth a whole litter," Timothy says as he logs in the birth order and times into the computer.

"That's all? The answer is a simple yes. Timothy, believe me when I tell you, there is nothing that Sean's magic can't do," Tien answers.

May 17, 10 a.m.

It's a little over a week before Sean is able to shift back into human form. The cubs are asleep in a pile as his limbs slowly stretch out and the fur covering them recedes. Carefully extracting himself from the nest, Sean makes his way to the bathroom. He has never stayed shifted that long and the taste of week old meat has him close to heaving.

Mouthwash will have to come first, and he refuses to consider the fact that one corner of their bedroom had been designated as the toilet as he relieves himself. He almost leaps out of his skin when DeMatteo's voice calls his name. Spitting out the rinse, he quickly wipes his mouth as DeMatteo grabs the Listerine, copying his routine. He pisses, quickly spitting and washing his hands before pulling Sean in close.

"Hey," Sean whispers, pressing a quick chaste kiss to DeMatteo's lips.

"Hey yourself. How are you feeling?" DeMatteo asks, making Sean realize that he hasn't taken any time to look at his body, now that he is no longer pregnant.

Where skin was once smooth, Sean now rubs his hands down what could only be called a pouch. He is pleasantly surprised by the lack of pain he thought he would be experiencing, although he can remember the excruciating pain he had felt during the delivery.

"Amazingly, I feel fine. There isn't even a single stretch mark," Sean answers, rubbing his hands over the smooth skin. He can't help but be mildly disappointed that he has no physical reminders of the most amazing thing he has ever experienced.

"Your lioness would have healed that. Did you want them?" DeMatteo asks, his hands joining Sean's.

"Maybe," Sean admits, enjoying the attention.

"Well, next time you will have to will the lioness to let some stay," DeMatteo answers easily and Sean laughs.

"Next time? Oh I don't know if I'd let you talk me into a next time. That was horrible. As a matter of fact, I need to call my mother and apologize, maybe send her flowers or something."

"I have my methods. So have you decided on the names?" DeMatteo asks steering the conversation back to safer subjects.

"Nice deflection, counsel, but yes, I was thinking Tiberius Matteo for the first born, Gaius Franklin for the second born, and for the youngest, Alexander Richard."

May 25, 3 p.m.

"DeMatteo!" Sean calls frantically for his mate.

DeMatteo races into the den, already half-shifted and looking wild when he spots his mate on the floor with all three cubs. "What's wrong?"

"DeMatteo, they opened their eyes! I thought you said… I thought they always…" Sean stammers. DeMatteo grabs his shoulders pulling him close.

"It's okay, mate. They are a little over two weeks. It's time for them to open their eyes," DeMatteo comforts.

"No! DeMatteo, you're not listening. Their eyes, look at their eyes," Sean insists pushing the Alpha away.

DeMatteo studies him for a minute. He knows that Sean has been insanely protective, but this is starting to get ridiculous. Deciding it is just easier to humor his mate, DeMatteo gets on the floor with his cubs.

The cubs all have their eyes open, and they are a startling shade of gray, but there is no reason for Sean to be upset. He is just about to tell Sean that when Alexander flashes his eyes, and they shine Alpha red.

DeMatteo's eyes flash in response, and he almost jumps off the floor when Tiberius and Gaius join in, flashing their own set of Alpha reds. "What the...?" DeMatteo says, as the boys struggle to get to their feet.

"Exactly, DeMatteo. I thought Alphas and Omegas are born one at a time?"

"They are. I've never... I honestly have no idea what is going on. We need to call Timothy," DeMatteo admits as he pushes on Gaius's rump, steadying him on wobbly legs.

"And Richard and Tien. And your parents. I think we are going to need everything they have about the prophecy," DeMatteo adds almost as an afterthought.

Sean grabs his phone to call the others, the thoughts of what this could mean for his cubs and what he has learned of the prophecy running through his head. He explains to them that they need to come to the den immediately to examine the cubs.

His lioness rubs against his mind, lending comfort, and the fact that she seems unperturbed by the strangeness does ease some of Sean's worries.

Timothy/Richard ~

"This is amazing," Richard says while he holds Alexander.

Sean is struggling not to shift as the babies object to being handled by their Alpha Apex. Each cub's eyes burn bright red as they hiss and squirm away, and Richard finally has to compel them to submit so Tien and Timothy can inspect them up close.

"There isn't any precedent to three Alphas being born to one litter, but with your magic it seems as if anything is possible," Richard explains.

Timothy has taken this chance to give the cubs a physical examination; being an Omega seems to have a calming effect as each one appear to settle when he is near. The fact that no one can explain why all three of the cubs are Alphas takes a backseat as Timothy scribbles notes on his ever-present notepad.

"Physically, they are perfect. The fact that they are Alphas could explain why you have been so protective over them. In days past, other predators would try to kill any Alpha or Omega cubs they happened upon since they are highly valuable to the pride. So it was imperative that the

Alpha Pair, protected these cubs above all else," Timothy explains, finishing the exams.

"Do you think they will have magic like me?" Sean asks.

"That is hard to say. We know they were able to use your magic while they were inside you, but until they are older, it will be impossible to tell if they have magic of their own," Tien finally says after a few minutes of silence.

"Either way, these cubs will need to be protected. I refuse to let my children be observed by anyone," DeMatteo states angrily.

Now that everyone has looked their fill, the cubs scurry to Sean as he sits on the floor. As they burrow under his legs for protection, Sean slowly relaxes until something in DeMatteo's tone grabs his attention.

"Observing them?" Sean asks, looking up at his mate, but Richard is the one that answers. "Because of their uniqueness, it wouldn't be unheard of for the Shifter Council to want to observe them for any abnormalities."

"Which basically means, study them like some kind of lab rat," Timothy supplies.

"That will never happen," DeMatteo grinds out, his eyes flashing. Sean coos at the cubs, who are now whimpering in distress at the Alpha's angry tone.

"That is enough upsetting the cubs. DeMatteo, no one will be doing anything to your cubs. The Council will have to be informed of their Alpha status, but a reminder that Sean is the Alpha Guardian should put a healthy amount of fear in them. They might be curious about the cubs, but the fear of a powerful magic user will more than stay their hand," Tien says.

"Thank you," Sean offers, no longer interested in anything other than getting the boys in their crib.

His lioness is growing agitated with the thoughts of others wanting to be near the cubs. He sends a message to DeMatteo, who begins to usher everyone out the den, as he carries the pups to the corner of the den.

Once the room is empty, Sean strips down and shifts back into his lioness. It is easier to nurse in that form, and he feels the need to be able to protect them. The cubs settle in quickly, each rooting around to find a nipple and settling down for the night.

DeMatteo eases back into the den a few hours later. Sean can hear him tiptoe around the room before his mate's giant lion joins them on the makeshift nest. Sean huffs gently as DeMatteo curls his large frame around his family, before drifting off to sleep safe, and surrounded by their Alpha.

Chapter 14

Sara ~ July 1, 12 p.m.

"We are going in tonight. I don't need to remind anyone how dangerous this is. I am going to need you four to keep the pride distracted while I get rid of the last two members of Sean's coven. Once I am off pride lands, I will call Hugh. You can start small fires at random places to keep them distracted, but it is crucial that you do not detonate the packages until I'm on my way back to the pride lands. Any questions?" Sara asks.

The three hunters are quiet. Sara knows that they are not comfortable working with Hugh, but they have proven themselves to be loyal. Finally, it is Carl, who seems to be the unofficial leader of the three, who speaks. "Are we sure that they are going to take Sean and the babies to the warehouse?"

"Yes, my connection in the pride has confirmed that there is a safety area for the witch and his litter. While everyone's out looking for us, we will get the jump on them there," Hugh answers smugly.

David Santiago has been the perfect connection to keep Hugh informed with what is happening with his mate. One of the former Alpha's children with his former companion mate, David has secretly hated DeMatteo since childhood.

David and Hugh had become friends through Nick. And even though he can't explain David's motivation, Hugh would be a fool to turn down the man's help, especially since he somehow got himself appointed as one of Sean's personal guards.

"We will all split up before approaching the pride lands. Communications are to be kept to a minimum; there will be random patrols out. We know the witch has set up spells to tell him when anyone enters, so make sure you stay just outside the pride lands," Sara continues.

It's imperative that they get this right. There will be no second chances. Once the alarm has been raised, they will only have a narrow window to ensure that the shifters follow the script. Right on time, her phone rings with her father's ringtone. Nodding to the other hunters, she heads to her soundproof office to take the call.

"I'm ready. Our witch has made a space to keep the others. Make sure you keep the female drugged and gagged. Once we have her here, her magic will be useless," Chris says.

Sara briefly goes over the plan before disconnecting the call. Ten hours. In ten hours, Sara will finally go after what she has been waiting her whole life for.

Sean ~

Shifting is becoming easier. With the demands of the cubs to nurse, Sean is spending a great deal of his day in his lioness form. If he thought being pregnant and giving birth was the apex of weirdness, it was only because he hadn't felt the sensation of nursing three constantly hungry mouths.

They seem to only have two modes, sleep and overdrive, and right now Sean is hoping to burn off enough energy to buy him at least two hours as a real boy.

Sean watches in amusement as the cubs wander around the front yard. This is only the second time they've been outside, and it must look like a giant forest from their perspective. Tiberius has found a stick; it's adorable as he pounces on his "prey," his tiny growls sounding more like a housecat than a mighty lion.

Gaius and Alexander are hiding under a bush nearby, watching, their ears flicking with interest. It doesn't take long before they shoot out, tackling their brother as they tumble across the lawn. It's hard to believe that these are the same cubs, as they have grown exponentially over the last two months.

Their speckled coats have faded to the golden tan of the other lions, and they have gained control over their too large paws. Their play has quickly turned into roughhousing as they tussle for position. No one has ever seen three Alpha cubs related to each other together, so Sean is just pleased that so far there has been minimal bloodshed.

Growing tired of the game, it is Alexander who first comes to nurse; he settles in quickly, latching on before his brothers note his absence. If Sean could in this form, he would laugh at the speed in which the stick is abandoned in favor of not missing a meal. Timothy assures him that they will soon take to their human forms as they take to eating meat.

Not that he isn't enjoying bonding with his tiny cubs in his lioness form and rubbing their warm bellies as a human. He just can't wait to see the furless faces that are a perfect blend of him and DeMatteo.

Gaius is the first to go; a painful tug tells Sean that his middle son has fallen asleep on the nipple. Tiberius soon follows, though he spends a few seconds searching for space between his younger siblings.

As usual, Alexander is last; he may have been the smallest at birth but his insatiable appetite has ensured that he has quickly caught up to his brothers. Of the three, he is always the first to the table and the last to leave. They curl tightly around each other as Sean slowly pulls away from the pile.

"I see they have taken to being outside."

Sean's bones crack and shift as he changes form. It still aches, especially when he has maintained this form for a long time. He smiles at DeMatteo. Although he has grown more comfortable shifting and being nude in general, he really appreciates that his mate still brings out his robe.

"Yeah, they've been sleeping better now that they have more room to run," Sean answers, reaching up for his kiss. "So how is work?" Sean asks, pulling back.

The law office has been rebuilt, but DeMatteo still works his cases mainly from home. Since the birth of the cubs, Sean nearly has to chase the Alpha away from the den, even though he can't imagine what it will be like when he himself has to return to work. For now, Sean just focuses on his family, refusing to entertain some far away reality.

"It looks like the Cline case will be headed to court. I'll never understand how humans walk away from their families. But I don't want to talk about that. Tell me, mate. What amazing things have our sons accomplished today?"

"Fair enough. Well, I think I can safely say that the boys are completely housebroken, and Alexander has decided my tail is the perfect chew toy," Sean says.

"Luckily, we heal quickly. My mother lost part of an ear to little Carla," DeMatteo confesses.

"Luckily, I've managed to keep all my parts. But speaking of parts, where the hell does my tail go when I shift?" Sean asks. To be honest this is something he has wondered from the first time he saw DeMatteo shift.

DeMatteo just chuckles, shaking his head. "I have no idea, but then again, I was always taught to not question the magic that makes us what we are too closely."

Sean considers this for a second, but honestly, having a tail pales in comparison with all the magic he has seen. "Ah, well then. Can you keep an eye on the boys while I shower?"

"Sure thing, and before I forget, Mary was looking for you," DeMatteo says sitting on the ground near the sleeping cubs.

"Was she? Did she mention what she wanted?"

"Nope, and I didn't ask. I'm not too sure your friend likes me," DeMatteo complains petulantly.

Sean laughs at his Alpha. Mary has made it her life's mission to fuck with DeMatteo every chance she gets. Yes, in some ways, she is still pissed that Sean had hidden so much from her, but most if it is because DeMatteo was trying so desperately to get her approval.

"She likes you. You've just got to stop making it so easy for her to bust your balls."

"Easy for you to say. You're not the one she is always threatening to castrate," DeMatteo continues, making Sean snort.

"I'd never let her cut your dick off. I like it too much."

"It's my balls I'm worried about; she keeps leaving vet cards around the house." DeMatteo growls.

"Well in that case... I'm just kidding, babe. I'm sure your cock and balls are safe. She just likes being a bitch. She'll stop eventually," Sean finally says before walking into the house.

Chapter 15

July 1, 10 p.m.

Sean is tossing and turning beside him, but it's the small hurt sounds he's making that finally wake DeMatteo completely.

"DeMatteo, someone is on the pride lands," Sean whispers, his eyes shining brightly in the dim room.

"What? Where?" DeMatteo is already out of the bed and grabbing his phone. He places it on speaker as soon as Samantha answers.

"On the lands; it's like they are circling the perimeter. The wards are flaring but they are not crossing in."

"You got that, Samantha? I need everyone rounded up. Get David on the phone, I want four guards on my mate and cubs. We need to find them fast," DeMatteo barks out as soon as Sean finishes.

Whoever is sniffing around is spreading their scent. That will make them harder to track, but DeMatteo plans on having his pride come in from every direction.

"That's good, baby. Call your parents and make sure they are secured. Take the boys in the safe room. We'll find them."

David is at the door in minutes. DeMatteo gives him instructions before heading off to join Samantha. Sean is on the phone with his parents as the other lions get to the saferoom. They need to move quick to assess how much of a threat is out there roaming the pride lands.

Stepping into the living room, DeMatteo glances around at his pride. This is much different than any of the battles they have fought against other shifters. These hunters have shown they will kill indiscriminately, and the poison darts they use give them an unfair advantage.

"We are going to be searching the pride lands in teams. We know that someone is circling the property. They haven't entered pride lands yet, but I intend to make sure they don't. We will be fanning out in every direction, corral them together. I want everyone traveling in pairs. If anything happens, howl. These hunters are here to kill, so don't hesitate to put them down if you come upon one. Only kill if you have to, but protect yourself and each other," DeMatteo orders the others.

DeMatteo's lion growls just under the surface as he accepts that he may be sending some in his pride to their deaths. The fact that he knows they will go willingly does little to settle his thoughts; as their Alpha it is his role to protect them. But tonight they will be protecting each other as they face these hunters head on.

Samantha catches his eye and he nods. He will not be traveling with her. As his head enforcer, she is his best fighter. Taking the signal, they all pour out of the pride house, and outside, the others all break off into groups of two. Over five hundred shifters set off into the night to protect their Alpha Pair.

Sara ~ July 1, 10 p.m.

Sara sits in the darkness. Through her scope, she can almost make out what the witch is saying. Frank is pacing in front of the window; no doubt Sean is begging his parents to run, but little does he know that it's already too late.

She pulls the trigger the second the witch ends the call. The silencer muffles the shot, the dart hitting its target before she can even register the sound of the glass breaking. Frank runs to the witch, and Sara is already on her feet running to the door before he can find the dart. Kicking in the door, Sara laughs at his expression as she quickly pulls the trigger.

"Hello, Mom and Dad," Sara says to the unconscious couple.

It's hard to believe this is the same woman she ran down all those years ago, but she isn't all that surprised to learn that her coven worked in the dark arts of necromancy. After all, these were the people who helped those shifters kill her mother.

It takes longer than she planned to drag the two to the car. She makes sure the ball gag is tight in the witch's mouth. Even though the sedatives should work for hours, Sara isn't going to risk her trying some fucking spell in the trunk.

Once she has them securely tied and gagged, Sara grabs their phones, removing the batteries so any GPS device is rendered useless. Grabbing her own phone, Sara calls her pet. It's time for them to have a little fun.

"I have the targets; I'm taking them to a safe house. Keep them busy," Sara orders as she steers her car towards the highway. Things are going perfectly.

DeMatteo ~ July 1, 11:53 p.m.

"We're going in circles," Carla complains as they make their way back towards the scent trail.

DeMatteo hates to admit it, but it seems like whoever is out on the pride lands have set up false scent markers, sending all the groups on wild chases that only lead them to discarded bundles of clothing.

He is just about to suggest heading back to the pride house and calling the others in when the first call goes up, quickly followed by two more.

Racing towards Samantha, DeMatteo sees what has the others calling: fires. Spread out in the distance, patches of the pride lands are beginning to burn.

"DeMatteo! They're trying to burn us out! I smelled the accelerant before the first one went up," Samantha rushes out as soon as she sees him.

DeMatteo can see where a new fire has just begun, and it's obvious even from here that the fires are headed to the pride house, where he has his mate and children locked in a safe room.

"Jesus, they're headed for the pride house!" DeMatteo shouts, throwing his head back. DeMatteo partially shifts to allow his lion to call his pride back to the pride land. "Samantha, I'm taking your vehicle. I have to get to Sean."

Carla is already climbing into the driver's seat. DeMatteo climbs in and grabs his phone; his first call is to Sean's parents, but the call goes directly to voicemail. Cursing, DeMatteo shoots them a quick text, informing them of what is happening and instructing them to stay in their safe room until he comes for them.

The next call goes to Mary; she is, as expected, less than agreeable about being locked into a safe room. DeMatteo is able to keep from growling as she insists on rushing to Sean's side, as his lion approves of the human's obvious loyalty to their mate. In the end, he instructs his lions to drag her, if necessary, to the safe room.

DeMatteo is out of the car before it even stops moving as they pull up to the pride house. The fires are still burning and seem to be getting closer by the minute. He is furious that they were able to trick him and get so close before detection.

Chapter 16

Sara ~ July 1, 10:35 p.m.

"Did you get them?" Chris asks in lieu of an actual greeting.

"Of course I did. I told you my plan would work, and it did," Sara answers as she drives towards her father's compound. Sean's parents should sleep the entire ride, but Sara won't relax until they could get the mother secured so she can't use magic against them.

"Don't mistake dumb luck for invincibility. If you could ask Nick, he'd tell you that's a fatal mistake. Don't forget to bring the computers to the compound. Those codes have to be there somewhere."

"Sir, I don't want to risk the witch waking up. We can go back for the files later."

"No, I need those files now; we might have to move quickly if they figure out the parents are missing before we are ready."

"Dad, I…"

"No! This is not a suggestion, Sara. Get the files and get them here. You have at least two hours before those darts wear off. I don't want excuses; I want you to do your fucking job!" Chris yells before disconnecting the call.

"Goddamn it," Sara curses as she snatches off her earpiece. Swerving into a gas station, she whips a U-turn and heads back towards her hotel. Something just doesn't sit right about the whole thing in her head. Chris has been obsessive about her getting these files for him, and something about that sets her nerves on edge.

She heads straight to her room, not bothering to check on the two prisoners in the trunk. Their mouths are thoroughly taped, and she just can't risk some nosy passerby to see her "cargo."

Sara takes the steps to her second floor room and heads straight to the safe. She has printed off a copy of every file. As soon as this is over, she plans to pour over it in detail. Her father is after something, and she is determined to find it.

Heading back to the door, Sara pauses. Not waiting long enough to change her mind, she grabs the MP3s of the audio files she had found. They were the only things on the computer that had any kind of security. She had thought she'd found the mother lode, but they only seemed to be minutes from Council meetings.

Heading back to her vehicle, Sara's heart nearly stops when she sees a police cruiser parked beside her. She forces herself to continue forward. *There is no reason for them to be suspicious unless you give them one,* she reminds herself as she reaches the car door.

"Hello, ma'am," the younger officer greets.

"Hello, officers." Sara smiles at the officers. She feels a wave of relief as she notices the older cop's focus is on her ass, not her face. She makes sure to keep her body positioned to block their view of the weapons in the car. They are covered by a blanket, but too close of an inspection could be troublesome.

"That's a nice car you have there."

"Thanks, it's my daddy's. You gentlemen have a great day, and be safe out there," Sara answers as she slides behind the wheel.

"Thank you, ma'am. You do the same."

Pulling back onto the road, Sara laughs out loud as the tension she had built up dissipates. Sara starts the next file as she pulls onto the highway. There has to be something in these files for Henry to have tried to hide them.

She isn't exactly sure what she expects to find, but Chris's desperation to get his hands on the drives confirms her suspicion that he is after more than account numbers. It's not that she doesn't trust her father, but he raised her to never take anyone at their word.

These files are the only connection Sara has to the past, so there is no way she will turn over the only copy and trust her father to tell her the answers. Sara had spent hours going through archived files, but many of the older records were restricted to elders.

Once she is forced into hiding, there is little chance of any elder sharing their knowledge with her.

So this is it, the only chance Sara will likely ever have to find out exactly what the Council knew about the disappearance of her mother and why they were so quick to give up their search for her.

"Archive file six hundred and seventy-two, case of Melanie and Christian Mitchel." Sara is just about to skip past another boring meeting transcription when suddenly a name from her past grabs her attention.

The sound of her mother's name almost makes Sara drive off the road. She slows down and rolls up the window; even with the volume up to the max, the voices on the tape are not very loud.

"Before we begin this mediation, I must advise all parties that these proceedings will be recorded and preserved in the archives. You have agreed to having the elders mediate your petitions. Do you agree to proceed?" Henry says.

"Yes," Chris says. Sara recognizes her father's voice, although he sounds so young. She can also tell that whatever is about to be discussed has her father very angry.

"Yes," Melanie says. Sara thinks that is her mother's voice, although her memories of her mother are so faded that she honestly can't be sure that it's her.

"Yes," say four other men whose voices Sara can't identify. There are some movements and conversations she can't quite make out, so she skips forward to where one of the four other men begins to speak.

"Very well. Let's begin. I, Reynold Shinn, Head of the Human Council, and Alpha Apex Richard Santiago, have agreed to stand in judgment of the mating of Melanie Mitchel, human, and Adrian Duncan, Beta wolf of the Seattle pack. Our decision here will be binding and final. Henry Steinbeck and Alpha Matthew Santiago will stand as witnesses," Reynold says. His voice is loud and commanding, but Sara is focused on just one thing: her mother was mated to a shifter?

"Reynold, Alpha, I am asking to take my daughter Sara Mitchel into the pack. I bonded with my true mate today, and I wish to dissolve my marriage," Melanie states.

"I refuse. That thing mate bit my wife! We are still legally married, and there had been no talks of separation before she met him! I want him put down for breaking the treaty. What he did is forbidden and I demand repercussions!" Chris yells.

"Chris, you need to calm down."

"Calm down? Are you fucking kidding me, Henry? You've known me for years. Whose side are you on?" Chris asks.

"Chris, I am here as a witness. I'm not on anyone's side, but as your friend, I'm telling you to show respect to the elders," Henry responds.

"If you are done, Mr. Mitchel. Is it true that you have mate bitten this woman?"

"Yes, Elder Reynold," Adrian answers.

"If I may speak, Elders?"

"Go ahead. Please state your name and connection to this case for the record," Reynold confirms.

"My name is Alpha Robert Lee, and I am Adrian's Alpha. I am here to explain how this mistake happened. Adrian is new to the pride; he had been living in his wolf form for most of his life before he was found. We have been slowly introducing him to pack life and teaching him the treaty laws. This was his first week off pack lands working on our construction site. I never thought he would find his mate so quickly, so I hadn't taught him the mating laws. After his wolf claimed his mate, he brought her to the pack. Once she explained who she was, I called Alpha Apex Santiago before heading down here. If anyone is to be punished, it should be me for failing to train my young wolf properly."

"That is bullshit!"

"You will remain quiet, Chris. We will determine who will be punished," Reynold asserts.

"Mrs. Mitchel, did you consent to this mating? And did you understand the rules regarding mating?" Richard asks.

"Yes, I consented. When he approached me, I was instantly attracted to him, but it was more than that. He didn't just... He didn't just walk up and bite me, Chris. We talked for hours, and I knew I wanted to be with him. He told me what he was, and he asked me to be his mate, and I said yes," Melanie answers.

"This is ridiculous, you just met him. And now you want me to believe you're madly in love?" Chris sneers.

"May we see your mating mark?"

"I know you don't understand, but it was like... it was like magic. I can't explain it, but I knew I wanted to be with him the moment we met, and now I know I can't live without him. Please, Chris, I'm sorry I hurt you, but I need you to understand. It wasn't intentional..." Melanie pleads.

Adrian's voice cuts in, *"Alpha Apex, Elder, I beg you. I will accept any punishment, just please don't take me away from my mate."*

"We will meet in private and render our decision. Alpha Lee, please take your Beta and his mate outside. I will summon you when we are ready," Reynold says.

The MP3 stops, and Sara realizes that she has been driving on autopilot. She has no idea how she has gotten here, but she has to hear it all. It takes a minute of fumbling to find the next tape, and she realizes she is almost to her destination.

Sara pulls over. She is only a few blocks from her father's, but her hands shake as she listens to the tapes. Everything she has been told from that day forward was a lie. Her father, her grandparents... Everything they told her was a complete lie. She is finally learning the truth from her mother's mouth.

"Henry, can you take Chris upstairs?" Reynold asks.

"Of course, Elder," Henry answers.

"This is absurd; this is my house!" Chris yells. Sara can tell he jumped from his chair; the sound of it hitting the floor is unmistakable.

"Dammit, Chris, just move!" Henry hisses out.

"Reynold, this is complicated; everyone has gone about this wrong. But Adrian has broken the treaty. His ignorance is a reason, not an excuse, and he must be punished."

"I agree, although I believe his Alpha has had a part in causing this situation by not training him properly before setting him out on the population. What if he had lost control and attacked someone? This is why there are rules in the treaty," Reynold says.

"I agree. The Alpha also needs to be punished. I do not believe Adrian should be put to death. His crime is great, but the human consented to the mating. Condemning him to death could be a death sentence to her as well."

"Agreed. Now about the child," Reynold says, but *he hesitates.* There are sounds of papers shuffling and Sara wishes she knew what they were doing as Reynold mumbles under his breath.

"Yes, this part is the easiest. I vote that the child must remain with her father. This will serve as future punishment, but also it is unwise to have a full human join a wolf pack. No, I am not saying I think they would attack her, it's just that I know this child and she doesn't know that shifters exist yet," Reynold says.

"I will heed your judgement on the matter, Reynold. Although I want it noted that I believe that the father may be unstable. He seems to be extremely aggressive against

shifters, so I worry that he might in some way corrupt the child."

"Noted, but I assure you Chris is a seated member of the Human Council. He comes from a long line of hunters. His family name is highly respected in all of the communities, human and shifter. He is just in shock. It's not every day that you find out your wife is leaving you. Once he calms down, I'm sure he'll be okay, with the help of his parents."

"Very well, and I hope you are right. There is just something about the way he is reacting that is putting my lion on edge."

"When isn't your lion on edge when we have these things?" Reynold asks, laughing.

"Good point. We never have joint Councils for anything good," Richard says. There is noise in the background that muffles whatever Reynold replies with before the tape clears again.

"You ready to call them back in?" Richard asks.

"Yes, I'll call Henry on his phone," Reynold says. There are some muffled comments that Sara can't decipher before the others can be heard entering the room.

"After much consideration, we have reached our judgement. We have found that Beta Adrian Duncan has violated the treaty by illegally mating a mated human. You will receive fifty lashes as your punishment," Reynold begins.

"Yes, Elder."

"That's it? He steals my wife, destroys my family, and all he gets is fifty lashes?"

"Alpha Robert Lee, it has been decided that your failure to properly train your pack has resulted in one of your wolves being in violation of the treaty. Being that you are the Alpha, you will receive one hundred lashes."

"Yes, Elder."

"Melanie Mitchel, it has been decided that you were unaware of the consequences of your actions. As a human and non-hunter, it is not required that you adhere to the treaty."

"What!" Chris interrupts.

"Christian Mitchel, I will not tolerate another outburst from you. You are not only disrespecting me and the Alpha Apex, but you are embarrassing the Hunter

Council and your family name. For the last time take a seat and shut your mouth before I am forced to cast judgement on you!" Reynold yells.

"Melanie, being as now you are a shifter mate, you will be accepted into your pack. But, you will not be allowed to take your human daughter with you," Richard continues, seemingly unmoved by her father's outburst.

"No! Please don't take my baby! Chris! Chris, don't do this!" Melanie sobs.

"Being human, Sara is unaware of shifters, and it would be against the treaty to bring a child into the supernatural. This is the law, and now you are bound to obey it or suffer the consequences. These findings are final, and punishment is to be administered immediately."

"You have been sentenced by the Council. Matthew Santiago, will you take Beta Adrian outside to the vehicle? Their sentence will be carried out at the Shifter Council," Richard states.

"Alpha Apex, I want to bear witness," Chris demands angrily.

"Very well. Since you are the injured party, your request is granted."

"In that case, can the punishment be delayed until tomorrow? My daughter will be home soon, and I can't have her come to an empty house."

"Done. Sentences to be carried out tomorrow at 10 a.m. Alpha Lee, you and your Beta will be held by the Alpha Apex until your punishment has been executed. Alpha Santiago, escort these two to the cars. Have someone from your pride pick up their vehicles," Reynold orders.

"Yes, Elder," Matthew answers.

The tapes end, and Sara has to take a breath before moving. She can barely see straight from the rage that she feels. She checks her watch; the time her father gave her to meet him is almost up, but now it is her who is eager to see him. There is no time to really plan out how to get information out of the man so she was going to just play it by ear.

Pulling away from the curb, Sara can't help but wonder what really happened to her mother. If she wasn't taken and killed by shifters, does that mean that she could be out there somewhere, alive? But if she was that raises the question of why she had never tried to contact Sara, or maybe she has.

Parking outside her father's condo, the one thing she knows for sure is that Chris is the man with all the answers, and she will get them even if she has to break every one of his bones to get him to talk. She sits and waits as the garage door slowly opens, and suddenly the mission for her has changed.

The garage door creaks as it closes behind her. Sara opens the trunk to check on Sean's parents and immediately puts another round into each of them. She doesn't need any interruptions during daddy-daughter time.

"Took you long enough. What, did you stop for lunch?" Chris asks as he steps into the garage. Any plans Sara had about trying to ease into the conversation evaporate with the smug look on her father's face.

"So did you enjoy the show?" Sara asks, as she holds the pistol up high enough for her father to see that she is armed.

"What show?" Chis questions carefully.

"You know, I've always wondered about the story you told me. Things never made any sense. Everything was so neat, you told every detail exactly the same every time, and that was my first clue. But I didn't put everything together. I never knew how evil you really are until I heard the tapes," Sara says conversationally as she turns the gun to point it at her father.

She remembers how her father and grandparents drilled into her head how her mother was stolen: taken and probably killed by those animals when in fact it was her own father who had made sure she was separated from her mother. And right now she can't think of one reason not to pull the trigger.

"So tell me, Father, did you enjoy watching my mother's mate and Alpha get whipped?" Sara asks again as she presses the gun to his temple.

"Okay, baby girl, I'm going to need you to calm down. Put the gun down and we can talk."

"Or you can just start talking now," Sara answers, pushing the gun tighter against his head.

She points towards the house, indicating he should move, and Chris pauses to glance towards the open trunk. Leave it to him to be worried about following the mission, even when it's his life that is in peril.

"Don't you worry about them. I gave them another dose just to make sure we had all the time we need," Sara tells him as she points again with her free hand.

She keeps her eyes and ears open as they move through the house. No one else is supposed to be here, but she learned long ago to expect the least expected. So she doesn't hesitate to pull the trigger when T.J., her father's longtime friend, walks into the room.

"So where were we?" Sara asks, pushing her father onto the couch. She pulls a chair over to the wall and sits, watching Chris as he scrubs his hands down his face. He looks older and tired, nothing like the owner of the voice on the tapes.

"To answer your question, yes, I enjoyed watching those dogs get beat. They should have been killed for what they did to your mother. But I was foolish enough to believe I would get justice from the Council, which had turned into nothing more than the shifters' puppets."

"What they did? Dad, I heard her. I heard her with her own voice tell you that she wanted to go, and she wanted to take me with her."

"Yes, you heard her, but you didn't see her. You know what powerful magic they have. Just look at what Sean was able to do to you. She was under some kind of spell. If you would have seen her like me and your grandparents did, you would know that she was taken."

"I don't believe you."

"I have proof! It took me months to find it, but I had finally tracked down the evidence to prove she had been taken. That is why I need Henry's files. I gave him the evidence and he took it to the Council. When we went to confront the pack, they were gone. Your mother was gone.

Your grandparents found out that the Santiago pride had helped them escape, which is why we went there."

"So why didn't the Council keep looking for her? Why did you lie to me?"

"I believe the Council helped them escape. It's the only thing that makes sense. Why would they up and leave unless someone tipped them off? You know I am telling the truth; you've seen the archives. There was a wolf pack here in Seattle that just disappeared. Check the dates, you will see I'm not lying."

"Why didn't you tell me the truth?"

"What was I supposed to tell you? That your mother was most likely being used as a pack sex toy? That I had trusted the wrong people and probably got your mother killed? Or maybe I should have admitted that I was too weak to protect our family? Is that what you think I should have told my five-year-old daughter?" Chris screams, his face twisted in fury.

"Dad?" Sara cries, lowering the gun before dropping it to the floor. She can't begin to understand why her father never told her the truth, but she knows that he has never stopped looking, never stopped hoping, to find her mother, and that is the most important truth.

"It's okay, baby girl. I should have told you when you got older but by then... By then, I guess I just didn't want to admit that I'd made so many mistakes. Mistakes that have cost you dearly, but now, now we finally have the chance to get them. We will make them pay."

"I'm sorry," Sara sobs as she practically climbs in her father's lap.

"Shhh... baby girl, it's okay. I'm the one that's sorry," Chris whispers, and Sara can feel his tears on her shoulder.

"It's just, I heard those tapes, heard what they said, and I... I just fucking lost it, I'm sorry I didn't trust you," Sara hiccups out.

"It's alright. It's all over now," Chris says, helping her stand. He hugs her tight, and Sara can feel what's left of her sobs wracking her body.

"You okay?" Chris asks, rubbing her arms soothingly.

"Yes, Dad," Sara says, straightening up. Regardless of her father's mistakes, Sara knows he has only done what was best, and now it is her turn to fight for their family.

"Good. Now help me get our guests in the house. Then you can make it up to me by going down there and bringing me back the Alpha's head," Chris says.

"I do have one question. Did you really need to shoot T.J.?"

"Don't worry about him, Dad. It was just a tranquilizer round," Sara answers.

Chris stops suddenly and looks at her. Sara tenses, not sure if she is about to be punished for shooting the man. She almost jumps when her father bursts into peals of laughter, but after a few seconds she joins in, the tension between them evaporating as if she hadn't just held her father at gunpoint.

It takes nearly half an hour to move the two limp bodies into the house and tie them to the chair. The chairs are surrounded by some kind of magic drawings. They meant nothing to Sara, but Chris assures her that once they are placed in the circle, no magic will be able to reach them or come from them.

Dealing with witches makes Sara nervous. The ones who run in their circles tend to practice some dark shit, and they always seem to build in some loophole in any spell they cast. But with Sean's magic, they are forced to deal with a coven known to deal with death magic, and Sara is not ashamed to say that they make her flesh crawl.

Once the deal is done, Sara heads back to her car to head back to the pride lands to meet up with Hugh and the others. Hopefully the hunters have been able to control themselves around Hugh. He is going to be essential to them getting away if they aren't able to kill the Alpha and Alpha Mate.

Sara is five miles into pride lands and one mile away from the warehouse when she makes the call. Hugh and the others had situated themselves in position to light controlled fires.

Now it is going to be pure luck if everyone stays on the path. She just has to set up the traps inside the warehouse before anyone gets there.

Chapter 17

Chris ~ July 1, 11:40 p.m.

Chris watches as Sara drives down the road towards the pride lands. He had always feared that somehow Sara would get ahold of those records before he could explain. He had never imagined that his own daughter would hold him at gunpoint demanding answers, although he should have. He did raise her.

He refuses to let this setback slow him down. He is so close to catching up with that pack. He knows that someone in the pride knows where the wolves are hiding, and one way or another, he will find her.

"What do you mean she mated with a wolf?" Vivian asks as soon as she walks into the house.

Chris looks at the stairs, making sure Sara has gone to her room. He hasn't figured out what he is going to tell her about her mother. How do you explain that her mother has chosen an abomination over being with them? Chris still doesn't understand it himself.

"Mom, please keep your voice down. Let's go into the kitchen," Chris says, herding his parents into the adjoining room.

"What is going on, Christian?"

"I've told you; Melanie met her mate. They mate-bonded, and she left. Reynold and the Alpha Apex came over, passed judgement on the wolf. He will be whipped tomorrow. I get to witness it, and I get to keep Sara. The end."

"The end? Chris, are you drunk? What happened to the house?"

"Yes, I am drunk. And I am pissed, that's what happened to the house!" Chris hisses through his teeth, trying and failing to keep his voice down. Now that they are here, Chris can't remember why he thought calling his parents was a good idea.

"Give him a break, Vivian. He's been through enough today," his father finally says. Not that she would listen, but Chris appreciates his effort.

"Absolutely not. I want to go with you tomorrow. Are you sure they didn't have her under some kind of spell?"

"A spell? Really, Mother, that's what you're going to go with?"

"First, you better sober up and remember who you are talking to. And yes, a spell. There are all kind of witches out there that would have no trouble putting her under one. Do you really think a pack of dogs have any morals if they want something? How was she acting before she left?"

"Normal! She was completely normal, except she seemed glued to his side," Chris answers as he thinks back to this afternoon. But just like a puzzle, it was like once his mother showed him the missing piece he could suddenly see what was really happening.

"No wait, she only cried for like a minute when they said she would have to leave Sara. But then he spoke to her, and she was content to leave with him. I think she is even staying in his cell tonight while he waits for his punishment."

"Good boy. Now does that sound like Melanie? She loves that girl more than life itself; do you really think she would just walk away from her?" Vivian asks as she starts cleaning the mess he had made.

"No. No, she wouldn't.," Chris says, his mind going a mile a minute as he goes over every second Melanie was in the house. The more he remembers, the stranger her

behavior seems. If only he had been able to put together the pieces before she left...

"We will have to get enough evidence, but we'll get her back, son. I promise," his mother says, wrapping him up tight in a hug before leaving. Chris goes through the house on autopilot, locking the doors and kissing Sara's forehead, before he finds himself in bed staring off into the darkness.

The next day goes by in a blur, they arrive early, and the wolves are brought out naked and tied to a post. The blows are brutal. They would likely kill a human, and for some reason the wounds inflicted fail to heal.

The Alpha Apex explains that he applied a substance that would make the wounds heal humanly slow, done solely to prolong the perpetrators' suffering. Chris makes a mental note to look into other substances that can hurt shifters.

Melanie refuses to look at him during the entire process, and as soon as her "mate" is released, she rushes over to him. They leave immediately after, without her even asking if Sara is okay. At first he is devastated, but it only goes to prove that there is something controlling her.

He spends the next six months researching the pack, trying to keep tabs on what Melanie is doing and trying to get her alone to talk. He is taken completely off-guard when he is served with a restraining order from Melanie. She has accused him of stalking and intimidation. He is counseled by Reynold to sign the divorce papers and to end his investigations.

After the court case, Melanie and the pack seem to vanish. Chris knows they are still local, but every time he heads out to find her, he hits a barrier and ends up back in his house. It takes two more months before one of his mother's contacts comes up with the name of the coven that have been working to keep him away.

This is the final piece of evidence he needs. Kimberly Herr is the head of a local coven, and they work for the pack. He takes everything he has gathered to Henry, as they have been friends for years. Even though Chris knows he doesn't support Chris's mission to find his wife, he is the only one Chris knows who can convince Reynold to look into his case.

One month later, the entire pack disappears in the night. Reynold advises him to let it go but admits he has no idea where they have gone. They just vanished, taking with them the only chance Chris had to put his family back together.

Chris is so desperate he tries to reach out to the shifters. He petitions for an audience with the Alpha Apex. At the meeting, the shifters all assure him that the Herr coven only works in protection magic. But Chris knows that that witch was behind him not being able to find his wife before they disappeared.

His mother comes to him late one night with a plan to kidnap the Alpha and Alpha Mate of the Santiago pride. There is little doubt that they would have told the Alpha Apex where they were relocating. Going after the Alpha Apex would be a sure death sentence, but his brother is another story.

Moans pull Chris back from the past; the witch is finally starting to wake. Chris grabs a chair and pulls it close to the circle, wanting to be the first thing she sees when she opens her eyes. It's hard to believe after thinking she was dead that the witch who had helped hide his wife was sitting right in front of him.

"Welcome back! I was wondering if maybe Sara gave you a little too much and you would die in your sleep. I'm glad to see my fears were unfounded. I'd hate for you to miss watching your son and that animal die," Chris says cheerfully once he sees Rebecca opening her eyes.

He watches in amusement as she looks wildly around the room. Chris reaches out to remove her gag, noticing that she instantly starts mumbling under her breath. He sits backs and smiles as her eyes bulge in what must be excruciating pain as the wards on the ground flare to life.

"Don't bother with any spells, witch. You'll only die if you keep trying. That pain you're feeling is the wards that are all over this room keeping you safe to handle. Don't fight it. I'd hate for you to die again so soon."

"What are you talking about?" Rebecca says. Chris is impressed with her ability to hide her pain, but this game was over long before she opened her eyes.

"That was quite the little trick you played, hiding your spirit in this poor person's body, but I know it's you, Kimberly. Or would you like me to call you Rebecca? At first I wasn't sure, but then I saw you with your coven. What are the chances that good ol' Frank ended up marrying two different witches? I didn't peg you as a necromancer. I thought you were a good witch," Chris taunts, making a show of it.

"I am no necromancer; my life was a gift from the Goddess," Rebecca answers bravely, staring him directly in the eyes.

"Is that so? Tell me, did you recognize Sara? She's all grown up from that little girl that ran you down, but it looks like she managed to get you twice. Wonder why the Goddess didn't spare you this time?"

"My role has been filled, the prophecy will be fulfilled. But you, Chris, yes I know who you are. You will die first; I have foreseen it."

"You have? Well then, tell me, witch. How will I die?" Chris jokes.

Rebecca looks at him, head raised high, as a smile spreads across her face before she tells Chris what the Goddess has shown her. "Painfully."

DeMatteo ~ July 2, 12:20 a.m.

Fires are blazing all through the pride lands, and he knows that the house will burn like kindling if the flames reach it. The only safe thing is to get his family to the unfinished warehouse. The others are out looking for the humans, but they need to move.

When the second fire had erupted, DeMatteo had begun sending out messages to the humans to get them into their underground safe houses. Mary had screamed that she wanted to get Sean, but DeMatteo ordered her guards to physically drag her if they had to. He would not allow her to be hurt; Sean would be devastated, and DeMatteo just knows that this is Hugh and Sara, and Sean is their ultimate goal.

"Sean, we have to go now!" DeMatteo yells, racing into the house. Taking the stairs two at a time, DeMatteo reaches out through their mate bond, replaying everything that has happened to his mate.

"Sean, I need you to take the children and get to the warehouse. Humans are trying to burn the pride lands. I sent a message to your parents; they are heading to their safe room."

David and Sean meet him at the stairs, and DeMatteo grabs one of the cubs. They are already partially shifted. Rage consumes DeMatteo as he looks at his frightened children. They are too young to even realize how much danger they are in, but their lions respond to the fear neither of their parents can hope to suppress.

"Is it Hugh?" Sean asks, climbing into the car.

"I haven't scented him, but I am sure it's them and the humans that helped them kill the Human Council members," DeMatteo growls.

They've barely made it to the dirt roads when loud explosions rock the trees. DeMatteo slams down harder on the accelerator; he has to get his family to safety and then hunt these fuckers down. Peering into the rearview mirror, he sees his mate clutching their children. David has his weapon out scanning the trees.

"When we get there, I'm going to leave you with David while I go search for Hugh and the hunter."

"DeMatteo!" Sean says, quick to object, but DeMatteo can't just wait for them to strike. He has to keep the threat away from his family. Not wanting to speak the words, DeMatteo floods their bond with all his fears, begging his mate to understand that he has to do this.

"David, I want you to lock the door, and no one but me is allowed in," DeMatteo orders. Grabbing the cubs, they head to the only place on the pride lands that Hugh and the hunters would have no idea how to find.

"Yes, Alpha."

Once in the room, DeMatteo goes to his mate. Even without their bond or his advanced senses, he would be able to clearly see the fear and worry radiating out of every pore. He wishes he could assure his mate that everything will end fine, but he will not lie or make promises he may not be able to keep.

"Just be careful," Sean whispers.

DeMatteo probes their bond. He can feel the love and worry his mate has for him, not himself; the only thing Sean seems to fear is losing his mate. DeMatteo gathers him into his arms. This man never seems to stop surprising him, and he presses a chaste kiss to Sean's lips.

"I will. Just promise me you will stay here. No matter what. I need you to protect our cubs."

"I promise," Sean says, holding him tight.

The calls from the pride bring them both back to the serious problem at hand, and giving Sean another quick kiss, DeMatteo pulls away.

"I've got to go. David, protect my family at all cost, brother." The last part he directs to his half-sibling who had been keeping the cubs distracted while they spoke.

"I will take care of the Alpha Mate and cubs," David replies coolly. DeMatteo almost questions his sibling's detached reply when Samantha's pain filled call fills the night.

"Is that Samantha? That sounds bad," Sean gasps, looking towards the door.

"It was," DeMatteo grits out, his lion pushing to the surface. Hearing that much pain from his sister has the Alpha desperate to find her.

But something is prickling the back of his mind, an ominous feeling he feels down to his soul. He has no idea why, but something is urging him to stay with his mate and cubs.

Sean decides for him when he flashes his eyes and all but growls out in frustration, "What are you waiting for? Go find her!"

Sean ~

DeMatteo doesn't even bother to strip before shifting. The cubs are together in the makeshift play area they had set up for them. More calls sound off in the distance, and Sean can feel his lioness scratching just below the surface, wanting to protect her pride. DeMatteo's lion races down the halls and is out of sight before Sean can turn the corner.

Looking out into the night, Sean only considers disobeying his Alpha for a second before closing and locking the door. He lays his head against the door, trying to calm his heart. They knew this day was coming, but after two months of nothing, Sean had almost allowed himself to believe that the threat was over.

Now he needs to get himself together and care for the cubs. Sean knows that the cubs share a strong telepathic bond with him and the Alpha, and his fears are bleeding into them. Taking another deep breath, Sean pushes away from the door, spinning to rejoin his family in the safe room.

Time stops when he locks eyes with David, or more exactly when his brain registers that his brother-in-law is holding a gun pointed directly at his head. "David?" Sean asks lamely, having no idea what to say.

"Don't do anything stupid, 'Alpha Mate,'" David spits out the title as if it's an insult, his eyes glowing a sickly shade of reddish yellow. "I should have been born an Alpha, and I would have if my father hadn't found his true mate. I would have succeeded him in death and inherited the pride, but no, your mate had to ruin everything. But now I am going to kill you and take your Alpha spirit, and after the hunters are done with DeMatteo, take what is rightfully mine."

The click of David pulling the trigger is deafening as fire races through Sean's system. Everything happens at once. He can actually see the flame as the bullet ignites and blazes down the chamber. His magic and lioness both explode into action, shielding him as he shifts faster than he can take a breath.

The look on David's face as Sean launches himself at his attacker would be comedic if the man hadn't been trying to kill him. The surprise is short-lived as David narrowly escapes being instantly decapitated.

David shifts as he throws himself to the ground; rolling onto his paws, he snarls before leaping back into the fight. Sean is ready when the lion hits him, and they both roll on the ground, biting and scratching at anything within reach. Sean goes for the other lion's throat but misses his target, connecting instead with his face and cutting a deep hole in his cheek.

He can feel the cubs calling for him, but he tunes them out; he needs all his focus to be on the older shifter. Using all the training DeMatteo and Samantha have given him, Sean circles his adversary, swiping out at the other lion and littering his body with scratches and bites, while still maintaining enough distance to render his counterattacks useless.

Sean grabs his flank, biting down hard until his teeth hits bone. David roars in pain as he swings out wildly with his paws, claws hitting their target and fur flying as he rips into Sean's hind leg. Sean rolls him, using his bigger frame to force the shifter onto his back. His attention is diverted momentarily by sounds of crashing in the safe room and his cubs' frightened calls.

David takes advantage of his inattention, aiming to get the upper hand. Pain flares brightly as David rips his paws down Sean, from shoulder to paw. He pushes back with magic; his entire body burns hot, forcing the other lion away as the smell of burnt fur curls around him.

Not wanting to lose the momentum, Sean strikes again, this time connecting with David's throat. He keeps up the pressure as David thrashes, not relenting until he feels the man's windpipe in his teeth, and pulls. His mouth is still full of flesh as David falls to the ground, blood spraying from his torn throat.

He spits out the remains, not wanting to consume the flesh, and pants. His lioness is yowling in victory, but Sean feels sick knowing he has killed with his bare hands. Not wanting to focus on what he has done, Sean shifts and pushes to his feet, eager to get back to his frightened cubs.

Sean limps back to the safe room. Blood is pouring from his side, but he has to get to the cubs. Suddenly, the scared cries of his cubs erase any pain that may have slowed him down.

Racing to the safe room, Sean calls for DeMatteo through their bond. As he opens the door, Sean's heart stops as he takes in the sight that greets him. The cubs have completely shifted; their eyes flame red as they try to stand up to the partially shifted lion poised to attack.

"Hugh!" Sean screams as his lioness pushes to the surface; no one will threaten his cubs and live.

"Get away from my children!" Sean snarls, fangs dropping quickly as he assesses the situation. Hugh turns to face him, his eyes wide and partially shifted.

"Well, if it isn't the witch I've been waiting for. Did you really think you would get away with stealing my mate?" Hugh says. His voice is high and crazed, but Sean doesn't have time to consider his words; he just needs to get him away from his cubs.

"Hugh, I don't know what crazy shit Sara has been feeding you, but DeMatteo is my mate!" Sean says, stepping further into the room. He lets his eyes shine Alpha Mate orange as his claws unsheathe and his lioness readies for another fight.

"No! He is MINE! And when I kill you and those bastards you birthed, whatever spell you cast on him will be broken!" Hugh shouts before shifting into his lion and charging.

Sean lets his lioness free, but Hugh is on him before the transition is complete. Sean's screams are garbled as

Hugh's teeth clamp onto his arm. He pushes back with his magic, forcing the lion back as he finishes his shift.

Hugh's lion is much smaller than Sean's, smaller than even David's had been. But what the shifter lacks in size, he more than makes up for with insanity. Sean had blasted him with a huge burst of electricity, and while it had forced the other shifter to release his bite, Hugh merely shakes it off and charges in for another attack.

Meeting in the middle, they twist mid-air, snarling, biting and scratching before falling to the ground. Sean easily pins the smaller shifter, flashing his eyes and hoping to force the other to submit and avoid any more death.

If anything, that just makes Hugh even more crazed. Sean is stunned by the pure fury that explodes from the smaller lion as he forces them both to roll. He twists his body quickly, keeping Hugh from biting down and holding him in place. It's almost dizzying as Sean finds himself now staring at Hugh's rear end.

On the ground they roll, Sean somehow ending up on his back. Hugh attempts to spin and Sean lunges and bites, his teeth grabbing onto the first thing they connect with, which happens to be Hugh's balls. Using his back claws, Sean digs into Hugh's belly, lifting the smaller lion completely off the ground. Sean rips through Hugh's belly with his claws while twisting his head, effectually disemboweling and castrating the other male.

Hugh's guts fall from his body, covering Sean as he drops the lifeless corpse. Rolling from under the deadweight, Sean immediately heads to his cubs, who are still whimpering and cowering in the corner. The sounds of feet racing towards them has Sean spinning in front of his cubs. He is weakened from losing so much blood from his two battles, but his lioness is bracing to face whatever new threat that enters this room.

"Sean!" The sound of his mate's voice, distorted by fangs, causes his body to vibrate when his partially-shifted mate runs into the room.

Sean's lioness is still wary, even though the human part of Sean's mind recognizes his mate. DeMatteo keeps talking to him; his voice is low and careful, Sean is both appreciative and annoyed. It isn't as if either him or his lion would ever hurt their mate. But with all the betrayals and everything that has happened, it is hard for Sean to calm his magic or lioness.

The cubs are whimpering behind him, eager to go to their Alpha, but Sean's uneasiness is forcing them to seek safety behind him. Finally, DeMatteo's eyes flash Alpha red, and that seems to speak to his lioness in a primitive way. Forcing the lioness to submit to their Alpha, the pain that he has been ignoring flares back to life as Sean lies down.

Reaching out to his magic, Sean starts chanting in his mind, willing his body to heal. He knows that even though he has killed David and Hugh, Sara is still out there somewhere, and as long as she is alive his family will never be safe.

Those thoughts are startling and scary, Sean has never been a violent man, but now he has killed two people in the last two hours. Both people had been trying to kill him, but still he can't deny that he enjoyed it, and that scared him.

Once he feels his body is mostly healed, Sean starts to shift back into his human form. DeMatteo is watching him carefully; he had seemed distressed by the extent of Sean's injuries, but Sean knows his pain will only be magnified once he tells him that his brother had attempted to kill him and was most likely working with Hugh and the hunters.

Chapter 18

"Sean?" DeMatteo says again as he approaches his mate. Sean is covered in blood, his entire body poised for attack as he stands in front of the cubs.

"Sean, it's me," DeMatteo tries again. Sean's body is shaking, and DeMatteo struggles not to look at the remains of his former lover as he tries to reach out through their bond. Flashing his eyes, DeMatteo exhales sharply when Sean flashes his in return before lying on his belly.

"Fuck," DeMatteo hisses as he sees the damage his mate has sustained. He can't help but blame himself for this. DeMatteo had just killed the hunter who had shot Samantha when Sean's call had slammed through their bond.

Samantha had lain paralyzed as the human was slowly attempting to remove her fur, and DeMatteo had lost it. The savage visual of his sister being skinned alive had sent DeMatteo into a blood lust, and he had ripped the human apart. He had still been tearing his flesh from his bones when he'd felt his mate calling for him. The level of fear flooding their bond had DeMatteo leaving his sister where she lain, still paralyzed.

The cubs are whimpering pathetically behind their mother, and DeMatteo rumbles at them, letting them know their Alpha is here and will protect them. Sean's lioness begins to glow faintly, and DeMatteo watches in awe as the wounds that are scattered all over his sides slowly begin to heal.

Shifters heal quickly, but these wounds would have required hours to heal on their own. Sean's magic is flaring brightly as he stretches out his newly healed limbs. The cubs are peeking at DeMatteo from behind Sean, still too scared to come out on their own. DeMatteo sits and extends his hand allowing the cubs to scent him.

Alexander is the first to take the offering, sniffing and whining, his eyes shining brightly as he slowly edges closer. Once they touch, their bond flares brightly, and Alexander yips before running to press into DeMatteo's side. The others follow quickly, each one sniffing the air carefully before running to their father.

"DeMatteo," Sean calls weakly as he shifts back to his human form. DeMatteo pulls away from the cubs, earning distressed whimpers as he crawls over to where Sean is lying.

"Baby, I'm so sorry I left you. I am so fucking sorry," DeMatteo apologizes. Something had begged him to stay and he had ignored it.

A decision that has left his brother dead and almost cost him everything. Sean winces, and DeMatteo knows his thoughts must be bleeding over, but he can't help it. He will never forgive himself for what could have happened.

"David," Sean groans, holding his side. The magic has closed the wounds but DeMatteo can feel that Sean is still in a great deal of pain. He must have used too much of his magic fighting off Hugh to heal himself completely.

"Shhh..." DeMatteo comforts, wiping at the blood that covers Sean's skin. Sean keeps attempting to speak, but DeMatteo starts to groom him, licking the blood off his face. He will spend the rest of his life making this up to his mate.

"It's okay. I saw the body. I didn't think Hugh would be able to kill him, but that was his job. I'm just glad you were able to kill him. I am so proud of you," DeMatteo continues when Sean tries to speak again.

DeMatteo is shocked when Sean flashes his eyes, pushing him away angrily. "You are not listening.

DeMatteo, David tried to kill me! He pulled a gun and tried to fucking shoot me. I had to kill him. I ripped his throat out with my teeth! When I came upstairs, Hugh had the cubs cornered and I killed him, too! Oh my god, DeMatteo!" Sean shouts.

DeMatteo is trying to make sense of what his mate is telling him, but it sounds crazy. Sean must sense his disbelief, because he growls again, partially shifting and filling DeMatteo with the memory of what happened.

DeMatteo almost vomits as he listens to his brother, the man he trusted with the life of his mate and cubs, explain how and why he was about to kill them. Then he is bombarded with the battle scenes, watching helplessly as David attempts to kill Sean.

Finally, Sean shows him his confrontation with Hugh. The man had become completely insane. DeMatteo is in awe at how his mate had not only fought, but won, two battles with much older shifters, one while severely injured. Once the visions stopped, DeMatteo just pulls Sean close; there is nothing he can say that will take away what has happened. The cubs, still shifted, climb in close, whimpering pitifully and pressing against them.

They stay like that for what seems like forever, but much too soon Sean is pulling away. DeMatteo reaches out to run his hands over the cubs, they likely will stay this way for some time. He purrs to them again, reveling in the affectionate pulses the cubs send through their bond.

"Did you find Samantha?" Sean asks.

"Yes. She had been shot with a tranquilizer. I dealt with the hunter, but then you called and..." DeMatteo answers honestly.

He doesn't want to share the more gruesome discovery of what he caught the hunter doing, not in front of the cubs.

"We should get going. I don't feel safe here. David must have told Hugh and the hunters about this place," Sean says, not taking his eyes off the cubs.

DeMatteo suppresses a growl. David had betrayed them in every way. That is the only explanation as to why Hugh lay dead in a place he would have no way of knowing about if DeMatteo hadn't been sold out by his own brother.

"Yes, I think we should stay together," DeMatteo agrees quickly.

Now that Sean has voiced his concerns, DeMatteo's lion is almost ripping through his skin to protect his mate. They need to get with the rest of the pride, where they will be safer in larger numbers.

Sean climbs to his feet; he must be still using his magic trying to heal his damage, and DeMatteo grimaces at the burst of magic that flares through his system. DeMatteo shakes off his guilt as they lead the children out of the safe room. He can spend as much time beating himself up as he wants after his family is safe.

DeMatteo slams to a halt, eyes flashing and fangs bared at the woman standing at the door, smiling.

"Hello, Sean. Miss me?" the woman asks, waving what looks like a hand grenade in their direction. DeMatteo starts carefully maneuvering his family towards the large windows before Sean can speak.

"Sara." DeMatteo's claws pop, and he growls as he hears his mate speak the name of the person that has caused them so much misery.

"Why such hostility?" Sara laughs. "If anything, you should be happy, seeing as you and this abomination have managed to kill the other two shifters. Guess it's true

what they say. There isn't any loyalty with you animals."
She tsks humorlessly.

DeMatteo ignores her insults, focusing on flooding
the bond with his mate and children and showing them
what he plans to do. Sean is quick to send back his distress,
but DeMatteo shuts it down, reminding him that his number
one job is saving the cubs. Their whimpers draw the
hunter's attention.

"Ah, I see you've birthed those things," Sara says,
taking a step forward. DeMatteo lunges, forcing her back a
step before she seems to remember her little insurance
policy.

"Careful, kitty. You wouldn't want me to drop this,
would you? I know you know who I am, and you know that
I will not hesitate to kill you all. But that is not what I want
right now."

"What do you want?" Sean asks.

"Not much, I just want dear old Matthew to tell me
what happened to my mother, where his family hid the
pack of dogs that stole her. Deliver that and you all get to
live. It really is that simple."

"Your mother?" Sean says just as DeMatteo states, "I have no idea what you're talking about."

"Oh you know, or rather your uncle does, and you are going to get it for me. Or you two will share the same fate as your parents. It doesn't matter to me one way or the other; I've long since accepted her loss. But my father needs closure and vengeance, and I will give it to him."

DeMatteo knows that no matter if he tells her anything, she has no intention of letting any of them live. There is just something about the way she is watching the cubs that tells DeMatteo's lion she is a very real threat to his family.

Sean and the cubs are now close enough to make it out the window. There is no way to know how much damage that bomb will do, but there is no choice. He will protect them at all costs.

"Sean, take the cubs and run," DeMatteo says through their bond before charging the hunter.

Sean shifts and leaps through the window, the cubs following closely behind him. Sara throws the grenade before DeMatteo can wrap his arms around her. The walls shake, beams falling and slamming down on his back.

"My father will kill him and those little bastards, mark my words," she says.

DeMatteo looks at the girl beneath him. He almost feels sorry for the little girl she used to be, but that girl had died long ago. Unsheathing his claws, DeMatteo runs them through her stomach. He just can't let her live. His cubs and mate will never be safe with her alive. Her nails break the skin as she drags them down his shoulders, trying in vain to escape.

"Your father will die, same as you, if he tries to come for my family," DeMatteo tells the crazed woman beneath him.

"Family? You mean Sean? I had him first. I will always be a part of him." She grins, blood staining her teeth.

DeMatteo's eyes light up, his lion feeling dangerously possessive. Leaning in close, DeMatteo whispers in the hunter's ear as he slowly pulls his claws free. "He is mine."

The hunter whimpers as he stands, debris falling all around her. DeMatteo refuses to look at her as he steps over her body. He decides to be the animal she accused him of being. Instead of a quick death, DeMatteo leaves her to die slowly, painfully, and alone.

Chapter 19

Sean wakes up slowly to the sounds of their sons snoring softly between him and DeMatteo. He isn't all that surprised that each one had shifted into their lions. After the attempted kidnapping and the horror of witnessing such gory violence and death, it had been easy to convince DeMatteo to allow them to sleep in the den.

It isn't until he is able to pull his eyes away from the sleeping babies, still in their lion forms curled around one another in their crib, that he notices DeMatteo silently watching him. Refusing to disturb the trio, Sean greets his mate through their mate bond.

"Good morning."

DeMatteo responds by sending a flood of emotions through their bond. Sean is overwhelmed by the utter joy, relief, and happiness his mate is projecting in response to having his family together and whole.

Sean can feel his lioness stir as he sends his own feelings of happiness, although Sean is quick to realize that it would take time for him to feel whole. The entire incident is too fresh for Sean to gain enough distance to process how he feels.

Even though he would never regret protecting his children, Sean is finding it difficult to process the sheer joy his lioness had felt as he'd ripped Hugh apart. Sean had never been a violent person, but the need he'd felt to kill the threat to his children consumed his entire being.

It had been the first time he'd felt every inch the savage killer some hunters believed them all to be. But unlike what Sara preached, he felt no desire to kill every human in his path. Once Hugh was dead, his lioness had become desperate to be reunited with her cubs and her mate.

"Why don't you call your parents to let them know that we have the cubs and everyone is okay?"

"Oh my god, DeMatteo! They have to be worried sick."

"They will understand. I sent them a quick message telling them they could leave their safe room before I brought you and the cubs in last night."

"What did you say? Never mind; I'm gonna call them. Mom is probably climbing the walls to come over herself," Sean says grabbing his phone.

Both phones go directly to voicemail, and Sean looks at the phone in his hand. His parents never turn off their phones. "DeMatteo, has anyone actually spoken to my parents, since you told them to go inside the room?" Sean asks, biting his nails.

"No. Why?" DeMatteo asks.

"Their phones are off; I can't reach them. Something is wrong. I can feel it." Sean is already getting dressed.

There is no reason for his parents' phones to be off unless something has happened. "What if the hunters have them? What are we going to do?" Sean asks, panicked.

"First, we are going to call Tien. Can you use your magic to search for your mother's magic?" DeMatteo says.

Richard picks up immediately, DeMatteo quickly explains the situation, asking them to come care for the cubs as he and Sean search for his parents. The cubs start to whimper in distress, sensing their parents' fear.

DeMatteo takes each of them out of the crib, offering them comfort, and it seems like seconds before Richard is at their den.

"Thanks for coming so quickly," DeMatteo says, watching Tien as she shifts quickly before joining the cubs on the floor. They scurry over quickly, damn near burying themselves under the giant polar bear.

Sean keeps searching for any signs of his parents. It's like they have disappeared, but his lioness paces in his mind, calling out to her missing pride mates. Sean lets her closer to the surface, partially shifting in hopes that she will be able to better focus their magic into finding his parents.

They've almost made it to the waiting car, Sean following blindly as his mate steers him out of the house, when he feels it. A wave of magic slams into him with enough force to almost drive him to his knees. It's his mother. She is calling to him, her coven, anyone. Before he can tell his mate that he's found her, Sean is assaulted with a new call.

"Oh god, please no. DAD!" Sean screams as he feels his father reach out to him; his spirit is so weak. *"Mom! You have to save Dad!"* Sean sends out frantically. They haven't worked on his ability to reach out telepathically to others.

Frank ~

"I almost got it," Frank says, continuing to pry at the ropes around his wrists.

Chris and his guards have been gone for hours, and this might be their only chance at escape. His wrists are bleeding steadily as he twists and maneuvers, trying to work the knot free.

"Just break the circle, Frank. I can get us out of here."

"Almost... Almost... I got it!" Frank exclaims, pulling his hand free.

Frank's fingers are numb and slippery with his own blood as he flops on the floor. His blood works well as Frank scrubs at the intricate drawings and symbols around them. He can hear Rebecca already chanting behind him, building her magic for the moment the shields are dropped.

There is an audible pop when it works, and Frank can physically feel the magic expand in the room. He knows he is in trouble because the constant pain that has surrounded him from the instant the ropes cut into his flesh has dulled. In fact, Frank can't seem to feel anything as his vision blurs before him.

Epilogue

He arrives on the outskirts of the pride lands; it's pitch black, but he knows better than to draw attention to himself with a light. They had planned the attack precisely, so he doesn't need to see to find the warehouse DeMatteo would have taken the children to during the fire.

Pushing open the doors, he is assaulted with the scent of blood, and there is little doubt left in his mind as to how this scene had played out.

Pressing on, Chris searches through what is left of the warehouse and finds two of his hunters are practically dismembered. Their bodies are so mangled that it's only the fragments of tattoos on their torn up torsos that allows him to identify them.

When Sara didn't call at the appointed time, he knew that something must have gone wrong, but never did he expect to see the horrors that are greeting him.

Lion calls sound off in the distance. They must have left just moments before his arrival, and that is all the persuasion Chris needs to cut his losses. He still has the Alpha Mate's parents, so while it seems as though they've cut down his soldiers, Chris knows he still has pawns in the game.

It's only by pure luck that he hears it. He is almost back outside when he hears someone calling to him. Standing perfectly still he waits, straining his ears to catch the sound.

"Dad!" Sara rasps out, her voice weak and labored.

Chris steps closer, into the light pouring in from the broken window above her. Sara's body is littered with wounds, her blood seeping out onto the ground in a pool around her. He can tell that she is not going to make it as he sees her hands clutched tight against her body in a feeble attempt to keep her guts inside.

"Sara," Chris manages as he looks at what is left of his baby. She is already dead; her brain just hasn't gotten the memo.

"Dad, it's pretty bad. I think I'm going to need you to carry me to the car."

"Sorry, baby girl. You're gonna have to stay here," Chris explains as he grabs both of his morphine pens from his jacket pocket. He may not be able to save her, but he damn sure can make her last moments as painless as possible.

"What?" Sara grimaces as he shoves the needles deep into her thigh, one after the other. The effects are quick, but they are working even quicker due to her massive blood loss.

"Your scent. They would follow it, and I can't get caught. I still need to finish the mission."

"But… Dad? You… You can't be serious. You can't just leave me here. I'm dying."

"I know, baby girl, and I'm sorry. But I am so close, I know you understand. You know the mission always come first," Chris explains, Sara knows this.

He has taught her since she was a little girl that the mission always comes first. He'd expect her to do the same if their positions were reversed.

"Dad? Dad! Pl…please... Help me," Sara cries.

"Shhh... it's okay, baby girl," Chris shushes her as he watches her eyes flutter, the drugs doing their job.

"Fuck you!" Sara sobs out, and for a moment Chris is looking down on the same angry kid who had stolen his car, determined to do a mission on her own. His face hardens as he stands.

"See, and that is how you ended up here. So quick to get angry, never doing as you're told. I told you being overconfident would get you killed one of these days. But you wouldn't listen. In this regard, you've always been too much like your mother," Chris says before turning around and walking away.

Sara's sobs follow him out, and it is only a few minutes before he is back on the trail to his car. Off in the distance the lion calls sound even further away as they head back in what he can only guess is celebration.

But they haven't even come close to winning. All they have done is ensure that he will not stop until he has wiped every single member of the pride off the map.

Rustling up ahead snaps his attention to the tree line where something is moving away from his position. He catches a glimpse of it and it is huge, but the way it is leaning heavily on the trees would suggest whatever it is, it's already injured.

Chris grabs his gun loaded with tranquilizers, not wanting to risk it shifting or calling the others for help. He moves silently downwind, knowing he has to keep it from catching his scent before he is in position.

Chris continues diagonally, getting ahead and off to the side. Regardless of what Sara may have thought at the end, he loved his daughter. And this abomination would be the first to start paying for the others' sins with its life.

He springs out, gun ready, only just realizing it is Carl. It looks like the redhead made it out alive, but judging by the blood pouring from his side, he did not escape unmarred.

"Don't shoot!" Carl exclaims, holding out his hands.

"Shut up! Fuck, I almost blew your goddamn head off," Chris hisses as he lowers the gun.

"Holy shit, boss, what are you doing here? The whole fucking pride is out here," Carl questions, looking around.

"Well then I guess we better be on our way before anyone heads back," Chris sneers as he heads back in the direction of his car. Losing Sara was not part of the plan. Without their daughter, Chris will have to find new bait to lure his wife into the open.

He had almost forgot the other man was there until he cleared his throat. "Chris. Um, about Sara…" Carl starts but Chris cuts him off. There isn't time to wait for him to explain. Besides... Chris already knows his daughter's fate.

"I know. I saw what those animals did to my baby, and they are going to pay," Chris whispers. He will need to get rid of this idiot before leaving the state. But first he has to go back and deal with the fucking witch. He wouldn't be the only person losing someone tonight.

Carl ~

"Did you hear that?" Carl asks, gun waving wildly as he scans the darkness. He lost his night vision goggles on his way over to find Sara and now he is alone in the dark with an old man.

"What..." Whatever Chris was about to say is cut off as his head is slammed viciously against the tree.

Chris falls into a heap, and Carl only has a split second to pull his weapon and shoot. The round hits between the partially shifted lion's shoulders, and Carl squeezes off another shot right as the beast goes to spin around. That one goes in its belly, and Carl almost laughs at the way its eyes round in surprise.

The paralytic, tranquilizing shot works almost instantly; only the faintest hint of a howl was heard before it slumped on top of Chris. The adrenaline pumping through his veins keeps Carl from freezing up. Instead, he rushes over and rolls the lion to the side and checks Chris.

The wound on the old man's head is deep, exposing a chunk of skull, but the older hunter is still breathing. Carl goes to grab him and notices that the shifter's claws also opened a large gash on his chest. He doesn't have time to be gentle as he grabs the other man and pulls. If they have any chance of surviving, he has to get them to the car.

"Ahhh," Chris hisses out in pain as his legs drag the ground.

"Shit, man, you're hurt bad. I gotta get you to the doctor."

"No… got… gotta... get parents…" Chris's words are jumbled and Carl knows that the head injury is severe. And where the fuck is the car? His side screams in agony from the weight of the other hunter, but Carl refuses to die in these fucking woods.

Finally, he sees it just over the embankment, and Carl moves just a little faster. It takes a few awkward seconds of searching the other man as he moans in pain. Once he finds the keys he lays Chris down as gently as he can, before climbing behind the wheel.

"Where?" Chris moans out as Carl pulls out on the road.

"Nevada. I know a doctor there that will fix you up."

"No… house... Parents…" Chris pants out.

He is not making any sense, and Carl is relieved when the older man finally passes out. He just needs to get them out of the city as fast as possible. As soon as he gets far enough away, he'll stop and dress their wounds. But for now he just wants to put as much distance between them and the pride as humanly possible.

To Be Continued…

About the Author

Sharon Johnson is the pen name for a natural born story teller. The youngest of five, Sharon found the art of creating tales that had her parents often wondering if her adventures were real. Born and raised in New York City, Sharon spent most of her after school hours curled up with a book. An avid reader from childhood young Sharon took to expanding on her favorite stories, creating fan fictions. A former United States Marine she has a quick wit and a vocabulary that would make most sailors blush. Sharon spends most of her days as an ordinary electronics technician. If by ordinary you mean a heavily tattooed, pierced, and fiery redhead.

Sharon now resides in the beautiful Pocono Mountains with her husband, four children, two dogs, and two cats. She sets out every day to prove that you can never have too much on your plate if you love what you do. Mostly Sharon is a believer in love no matter what form you find it in. She specializes in M/M with Alpha males who are complex and flawed but are willing to fight for their HEA.

Word of mouth is vital for any author. If you enjoyed this book please leave a review where you purchased it, on Goodreads, or post it on your social media site. Sharon spends most of her nights writing but would love to hear from you.

You can email her:
mail.sharonjohnson@sharonjohnsonauthor.com

You can find her on Facebook:
Facebook.com/SharonJohnson1979

You can Tweet her: Twitter.com/SJohnson_Author

Visit her website: www.SharonJohnsonAuthor.com

Check her blog:
http://sharonjohnsonauthor.com/blog.html

Visit her on Instagram:
www.instagram.com/sharondjohnson

Sign up for Sharon's monthly newsletter. Get sneak peeks, deleted scenes, be the first to know future release dates, first glance at cover reveals, a chance to receive free ARC's, join her beta team, and so much more!

Also Available

Beyond a Reasonable Doubt

Book 1 of the Doubt Series

DeMatteo Santiago is the Alpha of one of the largest prides in North America. He is a young, successful lion shifter, surrounded by a large family and his devoted lover. By anyone's account he has more than any one man can ask for, but his lion cares of nothing except finding their mate.

An unexpected business trip pits DeMatteo and his long awaited mate on opposite sides of the courtroom. But when challenged by ex-lovers, nosey siblings, and crazy hunters, DeMatteo realizes that finding his mate was the easy part. The real question is whether they will live long enough to be together.

This release is an M/M paranormal shifter romance. This series will contain, graphic violence, graphic language, and Mpreg. What it will not be is an instant mate fairytale, as forces set out to destroy everything and everyone.

Erasing All Doubt

(Alphas Rule)

Book 0.5 of the Doubt Series

Eighty-six thousand, four hundred seconds. One thousand, four hundred and forty minutes. Twenty-four hours. One day. In his twenty-five years of life, DeMatteo Santiago had often taken for granted how much could change in a single day.

When DeMatteo crawled to bed at 10:30 pm on May 7, 1980, there was no way of knowing how the next twenty-four hours would forever alter his life. As a young Alpha lion shifter, DeMatteo has left his pride in search of his mate and a pride of his own. But the fates have been conspiring for centuries to lead him to this precise moment in time.

May 8, 1980, 10:30 pm: a moment in time that will forever change the life of Matthew "DeMatteo" Santiago. Facing the challenges of being the new Alpha of the largest pride in the United States, DeMatteo must find a way to lead in the face of his own personal tragedy.

A League of Gentlemen

Book 1 of The Gentlemen's League series

Dominic has spent his entire life fighting and hiding. After leaving the Marine Corps, he is embarking on a new chapter in his life and cutting all ties to the man he was before.

He's in a new place with a new name. But some ugly truths from his past, truths he thought were long buried, will come back-- and these truths are refusing to be ignored.

Ladies and Gentlemen

Book 1.5 of The Gentlemen's League Series

Natasha Tsarsko is a CIA agent with a dubious past. She is second in command for a specialized unit of operatives that work in the shadows of organized crime.

She's built her career on capturing the worst kinds of criminals. In her world, getting close to the wrong person can get you killed. But what happens when someone she trusts wants her to risk it all?

Coming Soon

Only Truth Remains

Book 3 in Doubt Series

Philip Cooke is the Alpha of the Montana Wolf Pack; they have served as the head enforcers for the Joint Counsel for over a hundred years mostly because of their ability to remain neutral. But when a call from Richard Santiago, Alpha Apex of all shifters in North America, summons him to hunt down a rogue lion, his options of remaining neutral disappear.

Once in Seattle, Philip meets Alpha Mate Sean and Alpha DeMatteo Santiago, nephew of the Alpha Apex and target of the rogue lion's affections. The case takes a bizarre turn when the rogue lion is killed in a failed attack, but his death leaves more questions than answers. Talk of the true mated gay Alpha had reached the pack lands, but Philip had dismissed the talks as mere rumors. Now with the undeniable evidence all around him, Phillip has to reevaluate all he has ever known and sacrificed.

When all the players are identified, one of the hunters appear to be the lost offspring of one of his own. Soon Phillip will learn that his pack is more deeply involved in this plot than anyone had ever realized, and choices made long ago have explosive consequences today. The death toll rises, but the case is far from over. In fact, it seems to be headed even closer to home.

Coming Soon

No Man Left Behind

Book 2 in The Gentlemen's League Series

The trail heats up in the search for the mole hiding within the Hive, but in the game of espionage there is always another game being played just below the surface. New passions heat up and take center stage as we continue Dominic's journey to a new life.

Up and until a few months ago, Samuel Wright has never spent any significant time thinking about his love life. Although to be fair, few of his conquests spanned beyond a couple of sweaty encounters, and until very recently, he had never seen a need for more. Men, women, and everything in between, Samuel liked to think of his bed as a sexual United Nations. There was no reason to limit his options.

Well, that was true until a certain spook joined their team...

www.ingramcontent.com/pod-product-compliance
Lightning Source LLC
Chambersburg PA
CBHW072322280626
47159CB00027B/267